## About the Author

B. Lynn Goodwin owns Writer Advice, www.writeradvice.com. She's written *Never Too Late: From Wannabe to Wife at 62* (memoir), *Talent* (YA) and *You Want Me to Do WHAT? Journaling for Caregivers* (self-help). *Never Too Late* and *Talent* are multiple award-winners. Shorter works ran in *Hip Mama*, *The Sun*, *Dramatics Magazine*, *Good Housekeeping*, *Purple Clover*, *100-word Stories*, *Flashquake*, *Cabinet of Heed*, *Murmur of Words*, and several anthologies. A reviewer and teacher at Writer Advice and Story Circle Network, she lives in Northern California with her energizer-bunny husband.

# Disrupted

# B. Lynn Goodwin

## Disrupted

Olympia Publishers
*London*

www.olympiapublishers.com
OLYMPIA PAPERBACK EDITION

Copyright © B. Lynn Goodwin 2024

The right of B. Lynn Goodwin to be identified as author of this work has been asserted in accordance with sections 77 and 78 of the Copyright, Designs and Patents Act 1988.

All Rights Reserved

No reproduction, copy or transmission of this publication may be made without written permission.
No paragraph of this publication may be reproduced, copied or transmitted save with the written permission of the publisher, or in accordance with the provisions of the Copyright Act 1956 (as amended).

Any person who commits any unauthorized act in relation to this publication may be liable to criminal prosecution and civil claims for damage.

A CIP catalogue record for this title is available from the British Library.

ISBN: 978-1-80439-348-2

This is a work of fiction.
Names, characters, places and incidents originate from the writer's imagination. Any resemblance to actual persons, living or dead, is purely coincidental.

First Published in 2024

Olympia Publishers
Tallis House
2 Tallis Street
London
EC4Y 0AB

Printed in Great Britain

# Dedication

To my former students—especially the actors whose work and skills I still remember.

# Acknowledgements

I want to thank Olympia Publishers and James Houghton for championing this book.

Thanks to Janis Cooke Newman's Creative Caffeine Daily workshop for inspiration, Meg Pokrass and Marj Hahne for their insights into editing, and the members of my ongoing Shush & Write Group for valuing persistence.

Thanks to Robyn Schneider, Shanna McNair, Scott Wolven, and the group at The Writers' Hotel who gave me solid feedback on the first 5000 words of an earlier version of this story. Thanks to the members of the California Writers Club and the writing partners who listened to my opening and gave me encouragement as well as suggestions.

Thanks to the Story Circle Network WIP group for listening to my weekly sagas and offering validation and confidence throughout the drafting and editing experience.

Thanks to all those who contribute to Writer Advice, www.writeradvice.com, for allowing me to see the world through their eyes.

Special thanks to Mr. Husby, aka Richard T. Brown, Jr. "You don't lose until you quit trying" is wise advice. I often share it with others.

Thanks to all the Topps and the Browns. Family matters.

# Chapter 1

## Wednesday, October 2, 2019

### San Ramos High, Northern California

The earth pounded like a jack hammer. I dropped my phone and it bounced on the floor of the main hall at San Ramos High. As I grabbed it, the floor slammed into my feet again. That jack hammer was working overtime.

"Get in a doorway," a booming voice called.

I knew that, so I was surprised when the current Student Council President came running toward me. The girl he was with said, "Chill. It's nothing. A trembler—not an earthquake." I must have looked worse than I thought because she stared for a minute before she asked, "You okay?"

I nodded.

"You're Sandee Mason, right?" the Student Council President asked.

"That's me."

"I remember the assembly where you spoke about your brother last spring."

I nodded. Here he was, in the job my brother, Bri, had two years ago, and I couldn't help wondering if Bri wanted to tell me something or warn me about someone. He used to send me encouraging messages after he died – at least I thought he did – and I kind of hoped he was trying to get my attention now.

"Don't worry, small quakes just release the tension between the plates. The big one's further away than ever and it seems like it's over now." He pushed the hall door open for his girlfriend.

"Thanks," I called after him. My dad had told Bri and me that factoid years ago.

I grabbed my books and stuffed them in my worn backpack, then slammed the door, which made as much noise as the under-earth pounding.

I was already five minutes late for rehearsal. Not good. Ms. G expected her actors to be prompt, and that went double for the stage manager—me.

The quake spooked me. So did the Student Council President. From the back he looked a lot like Bri, but Bri went to Afghanistan and the body parts they could find came back in a box.

# Chapter 2

## Wednesday, October 2, 2017

### San Ramos High, Northern California

I sneaked into rehearsal, unnoticed, as Ms. G told the actors, "It was just a small earthquake—an adjustment of the tectonic plates beneath the earth's surface. The little quakes push the big ones further into the future, remember? Now everybody take a deep breath, let it out slowly, and let's warm up."

I picked up the promptbook, which she'd left on her director's chair. My heart was still pounding. When we were rehearsing *Oklahoma!* last spring, I wanted to stage manage more than anything. Stage managers cue actors, organize backstage, and run the whole show during dress rehearsals and performances, but I was only the assistant until the stage manager got drunk a few hours before the final dress rehearsal, and Ms. G asked me take over for him. What a thrill!

After Ms. G finished the physical and vocal warm-ups, and we were on the second page of Act I, running lines, I saw her cell light up through her pants pocket. "All right," she said into her phone. "Sandee, you're in charge. Dr. Henderson needs me in a parent conference."

"I'm on it." I love running rehearsals whenever I get the opportunity. The minute she was out the door, though, Jenn called, "Line!" Was she testing me or had she honestly forgotten?

When I forgot my lines in Advanced Drama, it was usually because I was preoccupied with school or my friend Diego's latest crisis. Or the fact that my older brother wasn't coming back no matter how much we missed him. An involuntary shudder rushed up my spine again. It happened whenever I thought of Bri.

I gave her the cue, "Don't make a noise."

Jenn stared as if I were speaking a foreign language.

"Don't make a noise. Your father's been…"

"Got it." A second later, her character, Mrs. Gibbs, picked up an imaginary spatula. "Don't make a noise. Your father's been out all night and needs his sleep. I washed and ironed the blue gingham for you special."

"Ma, I hate that dress," Rebecca Gibbs said. Maria Rivera, who's Diego's younger cousin and one of three freshmen in the cast," plays Rebecca.

Diego's been my best friend since seventh grade. I often think we could be more if he weren't so incredibly shy. Most of the time he hides behind his drums and makes dumb jokes, but he went out of his way to support me last spring, and besides, he's getting cuter every day, whether he realizes it or not. He sang in the chorus of *Oklahoma!* because they needed boys, but between working at his dad's restaurant and playing in his band, he didn't have time for this show.

Right now Rebecca was staring at the back wall. I turned around and saw the school's library, where we seated the audience when we performed. It was closed this afternoon. Bookshelves lined one wall. Computers lined another. Sun streamed through glass doors that opened onto a patio on the third wall.

A guy stood in the back of the house, wearing a wrinkled camo jacket. I gulped and my heart lurched into my throat. He looked exactly like a photo of Bri that came back in his footlocker. Same brown eyes. Same shade of tan skin. Same walk I remembered. He strode toward me, his right arm outstretched.

Gasping, I said, "Oh my God! Bri, are you...?" My heart did major flip-flops as I realized I was freaking out.

The boy shook his head and said, "What's your problem? I'm delivering a note from your drama teacher."

"What's going on?" a freshman named Tony asked.

At the same time Jenn blurted out, "Do you mind? Some of us are trying to act."

I shook my head. My lips flapped, but no words came out. Camo Jacket rolled his eyes and walked away, shaking his head.

How could I make them understand that for a minute I thought my brother hadn't died? That my whole world turned upside down, just like it had in the main hall before rehearsal.

The note said, I'm **delayed. If you finish the act before I'm back, run the scene. Thx, Ms. G.** Much ado about nothing popped into my head. There were people in the cast who didn't know anything about Bri.

"Where should we take it from?" Jenn asked impatiently.

"Your last line?"

Nobody talked. Everybody on stage was staring at me.

Embarrassed, I pretended to look at the script, and said, "Take it from the Stage Manager's last line and let's keep going."

The actors started saying their lines, but their acting was flat and amateurish. When Jenn called "Line" again I asked, "What happened to the acting?"

"What acting?" Nicole muttered. Thornton Wilder's *Our Town*, which is our fall play, includes a wise narrator called the Stage Manager who knows the future. So odd to have a character called the Stage Manager when I'm the real-life stage manager.

The role went to Nicole Lorca, who's doing her last show with us. Nicole is the star onstage. She'll get the applause. I'll earn a credit for my resume that'll look good on my college applications next year, and I'll have some authority for once.

"Exactly. What happened to the energy and objectives you used when Ms. G was here?" I asked.

"You try remembering all those lines." What was Jenn's problem? "Well?"

"When I have lines to memorize, I start right away." I wanted to take it back, but I couldn't. Camo Jacket's appearance must have messed with my mind. I couldn't shake the odd vibrations I still felt, and I didn't know if they were from him or the quake.

"Some of us have more to do. There's AP chem homework," an actor protested.

"And I have a job fixing websites."

"And some of us have PSAT prep classes," said Bradley Thorpe, who played George Gibbs.

"Doesn't everyone want the best possible show?" I asked.

"Of course we do," Jenn said. "Why don't you give us a break and stop acting like Ms. G?"

"Yeah," Tony parroted. Watching Jenn's onstage son suck up, I wondered if he had a crush on her. Why not? Half the school did.

"Let's finish. Then you can do your homework and go to your jobs and work on your lines for tomorrow."

"You're not our boss." Jenn turned to her fellow actors and said, "Guys, let's do this so we can go."

"Good idea." I quietly tapped my pen exactly like Ms. G does.

Nicole giggled, but my sarcasm sailed over the heads of most of them. She'd only called line a couple of times during her humungous monologues. Nicole lost a semester a year and a half ago after she got caught driving drunk, and a judge sentenced her to rehab. I didn't know her then, but she lost her credits for fall semester and didn't graduate with her class last spring. She'd proved herself over and over and had become a natural leader in drama. Her life was on track even though she wouldn't be off probation until she turned eighteen.

We settled back into rehearsal, and by the time Ms. G got back from Dr. Henderson's office, we'd reached the last lines of the act. "How did it go, Sandee?" she asked once the actors finished.

"Pretty good."

Jenn sighed, or maybe I imagined it. I used to think I heard Bri talking to me when he disappeared in Afghanistan. Maybe I only sensed his messages, but I swear I heard his voice, and today I couldn't stop thinking about him.

"Any line problems?"

The cast stared, and I said, "A few but we got past them."

After reminding everybody to practice for Act II, Ms. G said, "Sandee, I need to talk to you privately."

She looked worried. Had her conference with Dr. Henderson been about me?

# Chapter 3

As the cast headed for Starbucks or their lockers, I asked, "Am I in trouble?"

"Thanks for staying, Sandee. Ms. Bowen stopped me on my way back."

"And she told you about my grade in Algebra II?" I stared at dried paint splatters on the linoleum floor.

"So you already know. How are you planning to fix it?" she asked.

She's so short that I looked down at her, but she's a powerhouse when she's directing. "Work harder?" I asked.

"I know you want to stage manage, Sandee."

"More than anything." I couldn't look at her.

"But you must keep your grades up. Didn't we settle this last spring?"

Hard to believe I wound up with my arch nemesis, Bowen, for Algebra II after our battles in geometry last year. Yesterday she made me stay after class and told me my grade dropped to a "D," because I'd failed another quiz. At San Ramos High a "D" means you can't participate in activities. That would destroy me.

Earlier, before the earthquake, I'd asked Bowen, "How are you supposed to study for pop quizzes?"

"If you learn the material by doing your homework, you won't need to study for them. Try being in charge of your geometry grade, because it needs you far more than any show."

I hated speeches like that. To change the subject, I asked, "Didn't you have a talent when you were in high school?"

Her eyes went all soft and dreamy. "Talents are nice. They make good hobbies, but math is practical; you can earn a living with it. There's always a job out there somewhere, whether you're a cashier or an environmental engineer." I wanted to put my hands over my ears. "You can pull this up. Just don't skip the homework you don't understand. Work through the problems and find the solutions. Math may not be glamorous, but it's a universal language."

"So's music." Bowen needed a broader view of life. She should retire. Become a freelance insurance calculator. Work for my dad. Do tax returns. Most of all she should stop torturing me.

"Did you know that music uses math?" Bowen asked.

"What?"

"Three-quarters time? Four-four time? It happens according to a specific count. Music's not random. It knows and respects the rules, and only breaks them for a reason."

"Were you a singer?"

"Pianist."

It was hard to imagine this woman, who had lesson plans laminated on her desk, playing in the piano bar at Stan's Steak House, where we sometimes went on Friday nights. I almost burst out laughing. Instead I asked, "Why did you stop?"

"You can't live on tips, Sandee."

"Do you like teaching?"

"I love reaching my students. If I can save one kid from... Never mind. If you and Diego do the homework together, you can talk through each problem. If either of you still have questions, come see me before school so you'll know the processes before class."

"So I can still stage manage *Our Town*?" I asked Ms. G

"That's up to you. If you're doing *all* of your homework,

you'll get top grades on pop quizzes. Now go home and finish every single problem."

Since Ms. G still stared at me I asked her, "What do you think of Bowen?"

"That's beside the point. She knows you can bring up your grade, and she asked me to remind you to do your homework because I'm the last teacher you see every day."

"Okay," I said. "I'll try."

"You can do better than that. We both expect you to succeed. Stage managers need math as much as anybody, right?"

"Sure. Just don't kick me out, okay?"

"Do your best in math and it shouldn't be a problem," she said, sounding too much like Bowen for me to be comfortable.

# Chapter 4

## Wednesday, October 2, 2017

### On the Way Home

As I walked to my car—okay my dad's car—the sun was sinking behind the ridge. Diego leaned against my back bumper, wearing his dark jeans and a graphic t-shirt.

His shadow stretched across the pavement. "Want to give me a driving lesson?" he asked.

My heart thumped again, though the earth hadn't moved this time. "You know how to drive, and you'll be sixteen before *Our Town* opens. Did you feel the earthquake?"

"Didn't everybody? The guys in the band were hanging out here, and Aaron's drum set almost fell off the back of his truck."

Diego worked in his parents' restaurant, bussing tables and bringing the customers their water and coffee. His dad, a skilled chef, wanted his son to learn the business so he could deliver orders. Diego believed everything would be different once his license made him legal, even though his dad had plans for him to deliver food once he could drive. I didn't think he'd even have time for his band.

He asked, "How's Rebecca doing?"

"She's perfect for the role." I kept my mouth shut about our nemesis, Ms. Bowen.

"Can I get a ride to Starbucks?" he asked, zipping up his blue Gap hoodie.

"Why not?" In April, during *Oklahoma!* we walked over, but this was mid-October, and we were juniors now. Besides, I liked spending time with him.

I loved being behind the wheel. Loved being the captain of my ship. Send me on an errand—any errand. Just let me take the car, I thought as Diego and I fastened our seat belts simultaneously.

"You okay? You're awfully quiet," Diego said as I slid into a prime parking space after a woman in a Tesla backed out. "Did something bad happen at rehearsal?"

"Why?"

"What happened?" Can't fool him.

"Bowen."

"Is that dingbat on your case again?" he asked.

"Madame Dingbat thinks the world revolves around math."

He chuckled. "Poor Sandee. Need some help?"

"Yup, but your math is as bad as mine. I got an F and a D on the last two quizzes, and I have to pull my grade up on the next one. Otherwise, I can't stage manage, and you know I'd spiral downhill if that happened."

He put his hand over mine and asked, "She's threatening to pull you out of the show?"

"For what it's worth, she suggested you and I work through the problems together. So how about it?" I thought about telling him that Bowen, of all people, had been a piano player—that the two of them had music in common. Why had she locked that gift inside her?

We passed a crowd of seniors, the guys in football jerseys and the cheerleaders in uniform. They'd gathered around the biggest outside table and were drinking lattes and Frappuccinos. A boy I didn't know stood leaning against the brick wall watching them. Diego waved at him and said, "Sandee, that's Pete. He's new."

"Hey, Sandee." I smiled and so did he. His mellow voice made my insides tingle. He had this quiet confidence, like he was comfortable standing there, watching the world without worrying about anyone's approval.

"So you're new to San Ramos?" Lame! But what should I say? Why was it so hard to find the right words without a script?

"Yup."

"You like it so far?" I asked, wishing something witty or wise would come out of my mouth.

"Pretty much."

"I don't suppose you have Bowen for Algebra II by any chance?" Diego asked. "We're looking for a smart study partner."

"Sorry. I've heard about her, but I have Gibson."

"You're AP?" I asked.

"Yup."

"Wanna sit with us? Maybe some of your smarts will rub off on me." I sounded dorky, but he didn't notice. We went up to the counter together and ordered.

"So how did you wind up in San Ramos?" I asked Pete as I paid for my Frappuccino.

"My dad got transferred from San Diego."

"So, what are you into?"

He shrugged. "Hanging out. That's how I found Diego and his band. And sometimes I run, which is kinda like making music with your feet." Bri had been a cross-country runner. I needed to stop thinking of him any time someone mentioned cross-country or student council.

Maybe the Frappuccino made my thoughts go too fast. Caffeine did that sometimes. So did anxiety, but I'd gotten over the anxiety that manipulated my life after Bri's funeral.

That had been a horrible day with Mom sedated and Dad as stiff as a stone. Talk about disconnected. All I remember was hearing taps—so forlorn—and a soldier handing Dad a flag folded like a triangle and saluting. Dad saluted back and I stared at the gravestones that stood like soldiers in parade formation. Overhead a few clouds drifted in the sky, and I hoped Bri was perched on one watching the service. The adults were all wrapped in a web of sorrow and there was no room for me.

"Where are you, Sandee?" Diego asked.

"Thinking about math."

"Liar," he shot back. Like I said, we've been pals forever. Pals. I'm as close as he's come to having a girlfriend. He kissed me during tech week for *Oklahoma!* and a couple other times. I felt something, but he must not have. He's probably more interested in foxy chicks, I'm sure, but sometimes I looked at him and wondered, if not me, then who will your girlfriend be?

"Seriously, Sandee, what are you thinking about?" Diego asked.

"You know ... stuff. Pete, have you ever acted?"

"Every time I ask for an extension on my homework. You know—my dog ate it, my computer ate it, we had a family emergency." Pete grinned and took another sip of his coffee.

Diego laughed, but when Pete said family emergency, my heart dropped. Life goes on, but when would it stop hurting? As soon as I trusted my voice to stay steady, I said, "So, you're good in math?"

He gave me a funny grin. "They really pushed us in San Diego. Lots of Navy people live there, and teachers always said, 'Math is the key to your future.'"

"So do you think you could help us?"

"Show me what you're working on, and I'll see what I can do. You don't mind, do you, Diego?"

"We could both use your help," I said, hoping Diego would be more comfortable if the three of us were doing this together.

Diego shook his head. "I'm late for band practice. Come by and jam sometime."

"You're a musician?" I asked as Diego left.

"I'm a lot of things."

As I pulled out my math book, my whole backpack slammed into my lap. My cup of Frappuccino tumbled onto the floor, and the lid flew up.

Pete jumped up. "I'll get napkins." A second later his butt slammed back into the chair. We both grabbed the table, which rocked like a playground swing on steroids. Our four hands weren't enough to steady it.

Parents scooped up their children and raced outside. The table full of seniors next to us grabbed their drinks and ran shrieking into the twilight. A clerk behind the counter screeched, "Earthquake," and ducked under the counter, leaving us to fend for ourselves. Tables around us teetered and two of them toppled. Hot coffee splashed on the leg of my faded jeans.

Pete shielded my head with one hand and my shoulders with his other arm. Even though the walls threatened to collapse, warmth tingled straight into my heart. Pete knew how to protect a girl, and he wasn't afraid of touch.

The walls swayed back and forth with the rhythm of the earth, and my stomach churned. Was I about to meet Bri on the other side?

A picture window shifted against its frame and shattered. Jagged edges clung to the windowsill. When the earth stopped rocking, my voice shook as I said, "There was one of these less than an hour ago. What's going on?"

"I dunno, but we need to get the hell out of here. If you'll let me walk you home, we could do math at your house."

Still shaking I said, "Better still, let's take my car."

"My kind of girl. Want me to drive?"

I wanted to say yes, but my dad, the insurance agent, would have killed me. "Not today. Let's go."

As I drove, I looked for Diego, and when I didn't see him, I clicked on the phone and said, "I want to be sure Diego's okay."

"Sure," Pete said, without looking at me.

"I'm fine, Sandee. You?" Diego said when I asked if he was okay.

"Fine."

"You and Mom called within two minutes of each other." I could imagine him shaking his head.

"It's because we care. Differently," I added because I didn't want him thinking I was like his mom. "Glad you're okay. We're pulling into the driveway. Call me later?"

"Sure."

Pete and I climbed out, grabbed our backpacks, and walked through the front door of my home on Sycamore Lane. I called out, "Mom? Dad?"

"Thank God you're home, Sandee," we heard Dad say through the kitchen door. "You okay?"

"Yeah. I brought someone with me."

I pushed open the kitchen door, and Mom asked, "Did you two feel the quakes?"

"Didn't everybody? This is Pete. He's going to help me with algebra." Mom stirred something in a dark skillet. It smelled like her chicken and pasta.

Dad perched on a stool by the counter, staring at something on his cell. "It's good to see that you're taking action. Ms. Bowen called me while I was with a client." He sounded quiet rather than angry. He'd used that voice since Bri died, and I hated disappointing him.

"Pete can help me turn it around."

"I don't think we know you. Were you in *Oklahoma!* or are you in *Our Town*?"

"Neither one."

"He's new," I added.

"Welcome," Dad said and shook his hand.

Mom hadn't said a word. It was mid-October, and the holiday season is hard on people who've lost family members--especially the first year. Don't say the "D" word, I reminded myself. Depression…not Diego. "Can he stay for dinner before we go to work?" I asked so they couldn't corner him with a bunch of questions. Dad and Mom looked at each other, and he gave her the slightest nod.

"I'm glad you're making new friends," Mom said. That felt hopeful. Every time she shook off even a speck of her depression, I smiled. Some moms I know might have turned into helicopter parents or started drinking, but she tried to move forward even though her son was gone.

"Could we maybe eat and work in the family room while you two have dinner here?" Pete asked.

She filled two plates with here chicken and pasta casserole and broccoli, and I said, "Thanks, Mom."

"So, where's your family room?" Pete asked as he followed me out of the kitchen.

"How do you know we have one?"

"All these houses have them. Like San Diego."

I led him down the hall and we each took a few bites before I opened my math book. In half an hour—maybe less—I could graph linear equations for both x and y. Frankly, I thought all of those variables belonged in a laboratory or a sci fi novel, but now that I knew what to do with them, I felt like a college-bound young woman again.

Once my homework was done, I asked, "Wanna watch TV?"

"Too much homework."

"You must have lots in your AP classes." I walked him down the path until I was thrown forward and then back. A car alarm across the street blared. The front porch light flickered. "What the…"

"It's either another earthquake or aftershock," Pete said. He wasn't even fazed. "Ask your phone."

"Smart ass. Guess this proves you're qualified to work at Starbucks, right?"

"At last. A job."

The shaking had come and gone. I looked back at the house. No visible damage.

My cell phone buzzed, and I called out, "See you tomorrow," before checking to see if Diego had called me back. It was Jenn.

"Hey, Sandee. Are we still having rehearsal tomorrow?" she asked.

"Why wouldn't we?"

"Haven't you heard? We're in the midst of an earthquake swarm."

"Really? I heard somebody planted Mexican jumping beans under San Ramos." I've been told that sarcasm is unbecoming, but it pours out of me when Jenn states the obvious.

"I'm serious, Sandee. The news just listed a bunch of schools that are closing until Monday. Are we one of them?"

"Nobody said anything to me. Did your parents get an e-mail from the school?"

"I don't know. They're at the Children's Theatre. Mom's directing *Charlie and the Chocolate Factory* and Dad's running the tech. Tonight's dress rehearsal, so they won't be home until after ten."

That was a good sign. Everything was normal, except in her mind. I could imagine her twirling her auburn hair around her index finger. I never knew if she did it to look helpless, or she didn't know what to do when her hands were empty. She wasn't the kind to pull out strands or chew on the ends of her hair, but being alone while her house shook probably scared her. I didn't blame her a bit. "Did you feel the last one?"

"Yes, the one at Starbucks this afternoon was bigger. The drinks flew out of people's hands, and everybody ran for shelter."

"At Starbucks? Who did you go to Starbucks with?"

"Diego." I didn't mention Pete to Jenn. She'd go after him, and he needed a chance to settle in before he met the school's biggest flirt. "Why don't you call Nicole? Her mom hovers, and if anything's come from the school, she'll know."

"Good idea. Maybe Ms. G called her first because she's a lead, and she'll get to you later."

"Bye, Jenn." Half the time she didn't have a clue that she sounded like a brainless twit. If she looked like the rest of us instead of being so gorgeous, she'd have to engage her brain.

I went into the kitchen, and before I could open my mouth, Dad asked, "Is your math done?"

"And did you two have enough dinner?" Mom added.

"Dinner was great, Mom. Is there anything on the news about earthquake swarms?" I asked to change the subject.

"Just that they have no way to predict how long they'll last," Dad said.

"And that it's pushing the big one further away?"

"That's the theory. I'm proud of you for remembering that. Would you like me to check your math homework?"

"Dad, I'm not a child."

"And you're not working to the best of your ability. Hand it over, please." So I spent the next few minutes watching Dad.

"Do you understand this?"

"Absolutely."

"Can you explain it?"

He kept nodding as I told him how to solve for x and y. After I finished, Dad said, "You can invite Pete over any time. I like that guy. He kind of reminds me of Bri."

Pete was not Bri, but Dad looked so happy that I couldn't burst his bubble even though he didn't need a replacement son. Had he forgotten he still had a daughter?

"Is there anything about school closures on the news?" I asked again. The last thing I wanted to do was talk about Bri or Pete. The earthquake swarm felt safe by comparison.

"It's mostly west of here," Mom said. "Oakland, Berkeley, Hayward, San Leandro, Fremont. You know. Places along the Hayward Fault. Even though the schools are retrofitted, the people they interviewed sounded pretty shaken up."

"The school districts want to avoid lawsuits," Dad muttered. Always the insurance man.

"Guess I'd better finish my homework if we're still having school."

I went up to my room, which had a yellow bedspread, matching curtains trimmed with ruffles, and some white furniture that I loved when I got it in sixth grade. A rag rug I'd made to earn a badge in Girl Scouts years ago was still on the floor. Good thing the posters on the walls changed whenever I found a new rock star or faraway place that intrigued me. Otherwise this would feel like a museum of my middle school years. I had a bookcase that was filling slowly with romances and psychological thrillers and a desk with my computer on top. I plugged in my cell before I started my science homework.

I hadn't read a whole page when I stopped and texted Jenn. Then I erased it. The last thing I needed was a girl who acted like a pretty little sister showing me up. A brilliant big brother had been bad enough. "Didn't mean it, Bri," I whispered, touching the lapis lazuli ring he'd sent from Afghanistan.

I kept fingering the ring and reading the same paragraph over and over until I texted Diego to tell him Pete was really good in math. I couldn't bring myself to send it though. The last thing I wanted to do was make him think Pete was better than he was. Besides, I didn't want to bother him if he was rehearsing. I'd write a new message and send it when the light in his room next door went on.

# Chapter 5

## Thursday, October 3, 2019

### San Ramos

While I ate my cereal the next morning, I asked Dad if I could drop him at his office and take the car to school.

"Sorry, kiddo. You'll have to walk. The car will be at the Oakland Airport until Monday. I have a conference in Cleveland, and your mom's using her car to run errands for the antique store. You'll be okay without it for one day."

"Fine. Maybe I can get a ride with someone."

"The school is four blocks away. You can walk," he said in his this-is-not-negotiable voice. I didn't answer. I picked my battles with my parents, and this wasn't one of them.

Instead, I fed Spike. Then I looked into his soulful brown eyes and said, "I know, Spike. I miss him too," and let him loose in the back yard.

When Bowen called on me in Algebra II, I was ready, and she said, "Good job, Sandee. There's a lot of power in your brain." I let her compliment wash over me until class ended.

That afternoon, when I walked into the theatre, the door between us and the library was closed. While I waited for rehearsal, Ms. G pointed to two stage lights that now shone on the linoleum floor. "Can you adjust those before rehearsal starts, Sandee? Just take a wrench and refocus them on the stage. It will help the actors concentrate."

I slid the ladder under the two wonky lights, and climbed halfway up when the door swung open, bringing in a burst of wind and Nicole Lorca. She took off her Nike jacket and fluffed her curls, then saw me wielding a wrench at the top of the ladder. "Want some help, Sandee?"

"Sure. Can you foot this aluminum monstrosity?" No matter how hard I tried, the yoke on the light wouldn't budge, and I was afraid I might yank the wrench too hard and fall.

The cast drifted in, a few at a time, and I would have felt self-conscious, but nobody paid any attention except Tony, who looked smaller than ever from here. "You need a man's help with that?" he asked.

Nicole rolled her eyes while I said, "If I see a man, I'll ask him."

"Zero tolerance for bullying," he muttered.

I ignored him. Cast members took off their jackets and grabbed one last look at the script. Jenn stood by the piano pontificating about something. The ladder swayed, rocking on its four aluminum feet. A structural beam behind the lights loomed closer and closer to my head. I looked down and saw Ms. G gripping the edge of her desk. Actors screamed as they crammed together in doorways and under the proscenium arch.

The whole room shook, and a couple of chairs skittered across the stage. I swung away from the lights, gripping the ladder rails and screaming louder than when I saw Camo Jacket and went postal. I rolled back and forth, pleading with a God I wasn't sure I believed in, while the ladder swayed further and further.

"The whole school is sliding off its rocker," Tony called out. My wrench clunked down one step after another adding percussion to the chaos.

"Bri? Diego? HELP!" I screamed as I headed for the beam again. The next thing I knew, Ms. G was gripping the side opposite Nicole. I came close enough to see one light vibrating against the pipe it was mounted on. The other had dropped straight down again, spotlighting the floor. "Help!" I called out again. The clamor in my head was thunderous. Had a terrorist exploded a bomb?

Ms. G sounded far away as she called out, "Hold on, Sandee." Someone clinging to the proscenium arch chanted, "Sandee, Sandee," and the people around her took up the cry. With Ms. G, Nicole, Bradley, and Tony all steadying the aluminum monstrosity, its rocking slowed. My heart pounded anyway, beating like one of Diego's drum solos. Breathlessly, I gasped, coughed, and gasped again.

A minute later, Dr. Henderson's voice came over the loudspeaker. "All students exit the buildings immediately. Now." He steadied his voice. "Go to the front parking lot and check in with any teacher holding an attendance iPad, even if you are with a teacher right now. If you have permission on file to leave campus, go home. If not, wait outside for your parents to pick you up. Outside. I repeat…"

"You heard Dr. Henderson. Everybody out," Ms. G said. Below me, the actors who weren't still shaking picked up their jackets and backpacks. From the top of the ladder, I watched, feeling like some celestial creature. "Go directly to the parking lot in front of the school. Sandee, come on down now." Ms. G's voice shook just like Henderson's.

I lifted my foot. Nothing happened. "Can't," I whispered. The soles of my shoes wouldn't budge.

"You can do it, Sandee," Nicole insisted.

"Tell that to these feet."

"Can you move your hands?" Nicole asked.

I slid the right one down about an inch. Then I did the same thing with the left one.

"Now try your feet," Ms. G said.

Every nerve shook and a cold wind passed by me as I peeled my foot off the rung.

Foot.

Foot.

Hand.

Hand.

The soles of my shoes shot tingles into my feet each time they made contact with a rung. When I got to the bottom, Nicole put a hand on my arm to steady me.

"Good job, Sandee." Ms. G's voice cracked again. Had she lived in California during the Loma Prieta earthquake? Dad told Bri and me it closed the Bay Bridge and shut down the World Series. I wondered if Ms. G was as old as my dad.

Tremors ran up and down my legs and spine and neck. A throbbing pain pressed behind my eyes, making my head spin. I kept reaching for something to grab onto even though Nicole and Ms. G were on either side keeping me upright. The ground tingled through my Topsiders again, and I imagined the dirt and roots and maybe even bones buried beneath the cement. Hadn't this land once belonged to Ohlone Indians? Were any of them buried under the school? My brain kept banging around. "Did I hit my head?" I asked.

"I don't think so," Ms. G said. "Do you need to sit down?"

"No. I'm okay." I figured I was overwhelmed by anxiety again. Justified anxiety.

I stumbled over the leafy branches that had fallen off the old oak standing between the Little Theatre and our music room. For a minute I thought the earth grabbed my leg.

When we got to the parking lot, I remembered that Dad's car

was at the airport. Had he heard what happened? Had Diego made it home or had Bowen kept him after class? Had Mom been driving, or was she back at Alicia's Antiques? Shaky muscles vibrated inside my arms and legs. Could I walk home alone?

Teachers checked off the names of students who had reported in. Skateboarders whizzed past debate club members, football players huddled with cheerleaders and volleyball players, and the cast milled around with the newspaper staff and the mathletes.

Diego sat on the bed of Aaron's F-150, texting someone. I started toward him, but Nicole asked, "Where are you going? We have to check in."

I nodded, feeling more like an island than a person in all this chaos. Shouts between students, teachers, and parents jumbled together. While I texted Diego, a twerpy boy jumped on the cement. My cell fell out of my hands, and he laughed and pointed. What a little punk.

Jenn said, "Calm down, Sandee. You're shaking." She would too if she'd been through my ordeal. "He's a kid. Like Tony. They're wannabes." Sometimes Jenn didn't realize how silly she sounded.

Nicole said, "We need to be sure Ms. G checked us in." She led the way while adrenaline pumped inside my ears, giving me a pounding headache.

"Jenn, you can leave," Ms. G said, "but Nicole, you…"

"It's okay. Mom's here." She pointed to Mrs. Lorca, standing by her Camry talking to another mom. "We'll drop Sandee off. She needs to rest." Ms. G only said, "See you two tomorrow."

As we headed across the parking lot, I realized the truck Diego sat in was gone. "We're taking Sandee home, okay?" Nicole said as she climbed into her mom's Camry.

"Sure. So where were you when the earthquake hit?" Mrs. Lorca asked.

"In the theatre, footing Sandee's ladder," Nicole said as she fastened her seatbelt.

"Her ladder?"

"I was adjusting lights." My voice sounded far away, though I felt my lips moving.

Are you all right, Sandee?" Mrs. Lorca asked. "Should we take you to the Emergency Room?"

"I'm fine. Just shaken up. If my headache doesn't go away, Mom will take me to the doctor."

"Can we turn the news on please?" Nicole asked.

"Any news station," I added.

Mrs. Lorca drew in a sharp breath before she said, "You don't need to hear about this. Isn't it bad enough that you lived through it?"

Nicole and I made eye contact before she said, "Please, Mom. We're not kids."

Mrs. Lorca sighed. "If you really want to know, parts of I-80 are closed, and some high-rise offices lost windows and even walls. Imagine being trapped without an elevator."

Nicole reached over and turned Sirius on without looking at her mother. "Sandee, are you up for this?"

"Absolutely." I wanted to know where else the quake had hit. Was my car, which was technically Dad's car, still sitting in long-term parking, or had the pavement caved in and swallowed it when the earth erupted? Why hadn't Diego's text come through? Was Mom okay or had plates and glasses flown from the shelves, slicing into her face and arms? I couldn't shut my mind off or look away from the radio.

Nicole's fingernails made half-moons across the skin of her

tightly crossed arms. She'd been through trauma before, and she might be flashing back on the night she was arrested. That would be a whole different disruption than this. Worse, I imagined. I hoped she didn't feel alone or afraid to talk.

A news reporter said, "It was calculated at a 7.1 on the Richter Scale according to UC Berkeley's Seismology Lab. This long-anticipated quake rattling the Hayward Fault brought down chimneys, broke windows, and ruptured structures throughout the East Bay. It was preceded by a swarm of tremors over the last few days along with a sharp increase in wind gusts. Scientists, who once claimed there was no such thing as earthquake weather, are now reconsidering that assertion. According to a UC Berkeley seismologist, 'It's just too early to know whether this is a freak incident or a part of the climate change which is affecting the whole world'."

"We go now to Karen Alvarez reporting from Hayward High School, where students are waiting for rides."

"They needed a reporter in San Ramos," I said softly. "We're in the same situation."

"Shhh!" Nicole and her mom said simultaneously.

A trembling, high-pitched voice said, "For a minute it was like one of those mystery spots where gravity doesn't work. We were running cross country, and the sidewalk wouldn't stay where it belonged."

"That must have scared you," Ms. Alvarez said.

Mrs. Lorca muttered, "This is the big one scientists predicted. The one we always knew could hit the Hayward fault."

If a rolling sidewalk scared this cross-country runner, the reporter would love hearing my story about swaying on top of a ladder. "Which station are we on?"

"ABC," Nicole said.

I reached for my phone, googled ABC, and phone number. No one answered, so I googled "new "San Francisco Bay Area". I had a huge tip: Interview the earthquake.

Nicole noticed me punching the number and said, "Are y trying to get a hold of your mom? The cell towers are probably out."

"I can drop you at her work if you want," Mrs. Lorca said.

"That's okay. We're almost home." Busted! My cheeks were burning.

What if they didn't understand what I was trying to do? Nicole hadn't been up there, swaying like a bird on a tree limb in a windstorm. Maybe she and her mom would hear me on the news. Then again, maybe this was a stupid idea. My head throbbed too much for me to know, but I was sure I was a part of the story just like the people in Hayward.

"Thanks, Mrs. Lorca," I said as she pulled into my driveway. I grabbed my backpack and added, "See you tomorrow, Nicole."

"Unless they cancel school."

My stomach dropped. What would we do with a vacation in October?

What would happen to *Our Town* if the school closed?

What if it stayed open, but we couldn't use the theatre?

This could turn into something way scarier than a roller coaster ride on top of a ladder.

# Chapter 6

## Thursday, October 3, 2017

### Outside Sandee Mason's Home

As Mrs. Lorca pulled away, I stared at the front of my house. Built in the early 1960s, it was set back from the street and lots of shadows ran across our deep front porch.

The shingles looked fine on this side and the chimney remained on the roof. Upstairs, our dark green gables were undisturbed except for one that was flapping like a haunted house on a movie set. No broken windows—upstairs or down—at least none that I could see. Twiggy branches covered the Adirondack chairs on the front lawn, and the plastic ones were overturned. The ivy clung to its lattice next to the garage door, but Mom's camellias, along the side of the yard, now bowed to the ground.

Spike yipped and yapped in the back yard. When I opened the side gate, he came running as if to say, "Emergency! Call somebody. The world's gone crazy."

I bent down and said, "It's okay, Spike. Really." I petted his fur, rubbed his belly, and put my hand over his palpitating heart.

When his breathing relaxed, I hit re-dial for ABC News Now and kept hearing, "This person is not accepting calls." So much for phoning in news tips.

Then I remembered something my dad told Bri and me one night at dinner. "You don't lose until you quit trying." I had a story to tell. If nothing else worked, I could submit something unique, send it to all the networks, talk to the first reporter who got back to me, and let the other news outlets pick up the story.

Want to know how it feels on a ladder when a 7.1 earthquake hits? Call (925) 555-9057 for my story. I read it to Spike, shook my head, and hit delete. An IT tech could send that message, or a dental hygienist.

Ladders and earthquakes don't mix—especially in a high school theatre. Call (925) 555-9057 for my story. Spike's tail wagged when he heard it. I copied and pasted it into every news tip page in San Francisco, Oakland, Concord, Livermore, and Pleasanton. Then I sent my tip to the *San Ramos Patch* and the *Pine Mountain Gazette*, which are only online. "Don't worry, Spike. Someone will call."

He looked up, his eyes full of trust, which made me think of Mom. An earthquake this big was way beyond her current coping capacity. She'd made me put her and Dad on speed dial after Bri died, saying, "It's for me, not you." Dad and I gave each other knowing looks.

I grabbed my phone and a minute later, I said, "Hello, Alicia? It's Sandee Mason. Is my mom in the shop right now?"

Her voice was muffled, as if customers were nearby, but I thought she said that Mom had gone to pick up Dad.

"He's at a conference in Cleveland."

"He heard ... so ... him up." Our connection was impossible. Probably everyone in the valley was calling someone. I was lucky to get through. She said, "...messages" and then she was gone.

So I checked my messages. Sure enough, Mom texted: Please call. Dad heard about the quake once he deplaned. Turned around. Rerouted to Reno. Picking him up. You and

Spike take care of each other? Riveras are next door. Call me now, okay? Love you.

Of course it was okay. It was more than okay. She trusted me enough to treat me like I was as responsible as Bri. I clicked on Mom, and heard, "This person is not accepting calls."

I texted back. Phone lines jammed. Spike and I are good. Love you. "You ready to go inside, Spike, or would you rather have a snack out here?"

He bounced to his feet, circling me like he does before a walk. "Get your leash." I checked the news on my phone, which said, "Aftershocks Ripple Up and Down I-80." I skimmed and discovered that the quake had been felt as far north as Eureka and as far south as Fresno. Though the damage was centered in Hayward, the wooden buildings in a hundred-year-old Chinese town named Locke were damaged along with some of the original buildings from the Gold Rush days.

Another headline read "Elevators stuck" and the article said, "If your loved ones travel along the I-80 corridor, they'll be very late for dinner. Police and firefighters have put out calls to communities throughout the state, asking for support to quell fires and prevent looting."

Firefighters. I hadn't thought about that, but I remembered reading about broken gas lines causing fires after San Francisco's 1906 earthquake. "Hey, Siri, are there any fires in San Ramos?"

"Here's what I found," Siri answered in her cheery, oblivious voice. Links showed fires in Hayward, San Lorenzo, Oakland, Berkeley, and Castro Valley. At least they hadn't traveled over the hills to San Ramos. During October tons of dry brush and dead leaves would ignite if someone dropped a match. Everybody knew that. I let out a deep sigh, and Spike looked up.

"We're okay." I petted him in long, slow strokes. "Let's walk you before it gets dark." After fastening his leash and grabbing my cell, we started down the brick path that split our lawn in two, but the earth shook again and I heard noisy clattering, followed by a woman screaming, "No! No!"

The tremor was a small one this time, but at least half of the bricks on the Rivera's chimney tumbled onto the roof, then dropped on the porch, ripping leaves off the ivy clinging to the garage wall. Splinters of shingles tumbled. I glanced at our chimney, saw no damage, and hurried through the gate that separated our yard from the Rivera's. Diego's mom stood on the porch, her arms wrapped tightly around her body. "La chimenea," she moaned. She'd been here for years, but when she was upset, she reverted to the Spanish she spoke as a girl in Mexico. "Los ladrillos se están desmoronando."

"She's saying, 'The bricks are crumbling,'" Diego said as he came toward me. "Mama, está bien. It's okay." He put an arm around her, and I saw that her apron had blood-red splotches. I hoped they were nothing more than tomato sauce. "The bricks and shingles were probably already loose," Diego said to his mom.

"What can I…?"

Diego shook his head slightly. "She's overreacting." He turned to her and said, "You need to calm down, Mama."

Minutes later she was still gasping for air, and I was worried that she was hyperventilating when he said, "Sandee, you know it was only an aftershock, right?"

"Sure. Spike barely reacted."

"So could you get her anxiety pills? She usually leaves the bottle on the kitchen table."

I tied Spike to a post on the porch and headed for the kitchen. Most of Mrs. Rivera's counters sparkled, but broken cups from the shelves next to the sink were splattered across the drain board and I remembered those red stains.

I grabbed her pills and a water bottle from the refrigerator.

I was on my way out when I felt a rumbling beneath my feet like a Jeep bumping over the railroad tracks. A stuttering boom and a crash followed. Wind whooshed around me. "What the…?" The back corner of the kitchen was angled oddly as if a sinkhole had opened up and swallowed the corner. Looking up I saw that the ceiling had separated from the wall. I could see windswept sky through the gaping hole.

I raced outside and ran smack into Diego. "You okay?" he asked, taking the pills and the water bottle from me.

"You better go look at your kitchen. No wait! You'd better get away from the house."

"Which one?"

"Oh, Diego, the back wall… is… is… Don't go in. I don't want you trapped in there."

"What's happened now?" Mrs. Rivera called over Spike's barking.

I shook my head and gently shoved Diego toward her. She took a pill and knew something had happened to her kitchen by the time I got over there. "I don't understand what's happening. Is any place safe?" A gust of wind swirled through the sycamore leaves, making them dance wildly.

"Why did the quake hit our place and not the whole block?" Diego asked.

"Diego, can you take a look at the back wall of the kitchen?"

"At what?"

"Kitchen. Back wall. Just go." He needed to see it. I couldn't explain.

When he reappeared, he stared at me with fear in his eyes. Then he waved me over and whispered, "There's a gaping hole in the kitchen." I nodded. "She'll freak."

"Let your dad tell her, okay? Maybe you two should come over to my place."

Mrs. Rivera stared at her hands clutching the water bottle.

Her mouth moved, but no sound came out. What happened to the confident, bossy woman next door? "Is your mom okay?" I asked Diego.

He shrugged as he sat on the varnished wooden porch next to Spike. I sat next to him. Our feet rested on the steps. After a moment he said, "I don't know what to do for her. I'll bet she's remembering the Mexico City Earthquake in 1985. Her family lost their home. Fires started everywhere, and it's like the past has come back to haunt her. She overreacts—just like your mom."

I disagreed. Mom's overreactions happened because she lost her son, a much bigger deal than the collapse of a kitchen wall.

Diego couldn't read my thoughts and went right on. "Mom's whole family felt stranded and helpless. They thought the earth was trying to burn them alive. Her family came north in '86. She was younger than Maria. You'd think she'd put those days behind her, but today was like a trigger."

"Mom, do you want to go over to Sandy's house?" She stared at her son, not comprehending, which was odd since her English is as good as mine.

Diego repeated my invitation, but Mrs. Rivera only muttered, "¿Qué bien haría?" Diego told me she'd said, "What good would it do?" She was in shock, like Mom when we learned about Bri.

"Should we call her doctor?"

"Nothing he can do. He can't stop the aftershocks, right?"

"Right."

My phone rang, and the ID, said KTVU--Oakland. My heart flipped, along with my mood. I was scared for Diego and his mom, but maybe a reporter at KTVU read my message and wanted to hear my story. Maybe it would help someone. With a pounding heart I asked, "You two okay? This is important."

He looked at me funny, and I said, "What?"

"Nothing."

"Say it."

"It's just that sometimes you sound like seventh grade Sandee and sometimes you sound older than the seniors." Before I could ask what he meant, he said, "Take your call. There's nothing you can do here anyway."

"Is this the Sandee Mason who was on top of a ladder when the earthquake hit at 3:23 this afternoon?" a professional voice asked.

"Yes."

"This is Tia Wong. I'm an intern over at KTVU—Channel 2 in Oakland. You're Sandee Mason?"

My breath caught. "Yes," I squeaked.

"Your message says you were on top of a ladder in your school's theatre when the 7.1 Hayward earthquake hit. Is that correct?"

"Yes."

"How did the earthquake feel up there, Sandee?"

My nerves fluttered like butterflies as I said, "Everything kept rocking and swaying, and I guess I was afraid I was going to fall and break something. The ladder was like a roller coaster that had run off the tracks or maybe like riding a surfboard."

"And who else was there?"

"Nicole was footing the ladder. Our drama teacher was there and some cast members for our fall play. Our teacher came rushing over, and I know the wrench fell cause I heard it crashing."

"Do you know Nicole's last name?" Ms. Wong asked.

"Lorca. She's the lead in *Our Town*. I don't know what we're going to do if…"

"Sandee, could I put you on video chat so we can record this? We'd love to get you live on the air, but the TV vans are covering the story up and down the Hayward Fault so…"

"Give me thirty seconds." I grabbed my hairbrush, threw on lip gloss, and smoothed my graphic tee with the comedy and tragedy masks on it. Then I clicked on video chat and there was Tia Wong in the KTVU studio with reporters at desks behind her. She didn't look much older than me. I whispered, "Do I look okay?"

"You look fine, Sandee. You look like a pretty girl who's had a traumatic day. Where are you right now?"

"Outside. I came next door when my neighbor's mom started shouting because her chimney was crumbling." I couldn't believe I was talking to someone at a TV channel.

"There's a lot happening today. Do you think your neighbor could answer a couple of questions?"

"She's pretty upset," was all I could say. I'd expected this to be my interview. Mine alone. But she had a point. Why not put San Ramos on the map? It would be great publicity if the show weren't canceled. "I can ask her if you want me too."

"Maybe I could talk to both of you together?" Ms. Wong suggested.

"Sounds good." For a minute I'd been afraid that Mrs. Rivera's story might replace mine. I hoped there was room for both of us. Hers might be the better story, but I didn't want to wind up on the cutting room floor.

# Chapter 7

## Later the Same Day

### Sandee's Neighborhood

Mrs. Rivera said she didn't want to be interviewed, so Tia Wong went ahead without her. As soon as I got off the phone, I texted Mom, hoping she and Dad could watch my interview in Reno. She hadn't said when Dad's plane would land, so she could be waiting at the airport, or at a restaurant, or stuck in traffic. Was I being silly, or was this how they felt when they didn't know where I was? Maybe people felt concern when they loved someone, but I didn't have time to think about that.

Instead, I sent a text to the entire cast and Ms. G: **Free publicity about the earthquake with a plug for Our Town tonight at six on Channel 2. Forward to your friends.**

Spike still needed the walk we'd started before the Rivera's chimney crashed.

The sun sank behind the ridge between San Ramos and Hayward, giving me a chill. Everything seemed calm, but my stomach still churned. I bumped into a rise in the sidewalk I'd never noticed and said, "Siri, flashlight on."

"It's on," she said as if it were any other day. A trash can full of clippings had flipped over. We skirted around it, which took us into the swirls of dirt painting odd patterns across the pavement.

Dogs weren't barking, kids weren't running, and only one lone girl on a bike rode past us. We spotted a few lights in kitchens. Cooking dinner sounded weird on a night like this. Too normal.

As I dodged another clump of branches blocking the sidewalk, I realized that some parents might be stranded at work while their kids waited in smelly school gyms or in darkening parking lots if the gyms were considered unsafe. I wasn't the only one with missing parents.

The red sky turned purple and then gray before we got home. Dusk set in and I found our front door was shut but unlocked. Mom and Dad would kill me if they ever found out. Please don't let any burglars be here, I prayed to the universe.

"Hello?" No answer. I let Spike off his leash. "Anybody here?" I flipped the light switch. Nothing happened. Off. On again. Still nothing. Had someone cut the wires? Was a masked burglar waiting behind the kitchen door with a knife in his gloved hand? Spike stayed by my side instead of bounding toward his supper bowl the way he normally did.

I clicked on my phone. "Siri, is the power out in San Ramos?"

She said, "Here's what I found." Sure enough, our street was listed.

The last time we had a power outage I was in eighth grade. Mom told us not to open the refrigerator when the electricity went off because too much cold would leak out. Instead, she let us snack on crackers and cookies. That night was as windy as today, and rain pounded against our windows. Dad lit a fire in the fireplace. Bri and his best friend Rob were there along with Diego and me, and we all felt cozy.

Mom told us about a campfire they'd lit in Yosemite the first summer she and Dad were married. Nobody'd told them that wood-burning fires were illegal that summer. They were in love and didn't even know that the whole state was in a drought. Dad said, "We'd been looking at each other and not the signs in the park." Diego rolled his eyes when he heard that, so I did too, but a part of me hoped he and I would visit Yosemite together sometime.

Tonight's blackout scared me because I only had Spike with me. "Let's check the house," I told him. "Siri, flashlight on."

"I turned flashlight on." Her cheery voice gave me hope.

I moved its beam around the room, stopping at each corner. Nothing was disturbed. Cautiously, I pushed the kitchen door. Mom keeps our mugs on open shelves by the sink. They'd fallen off the narrow shelves, like the ones at the Riveras. Some were nothing but shards, but the Love you, Dad and Love you, Mom mugs that I'd made ages ago were thick enough that they didn't break. I couldn't say the same for my *Oklahoma!* mug—the one that the cast gave me closing night. It lay on the countertop in pieces, along with a graduation cup that Bri's girlfriend had given him.

"Maybe we can piece them together when we have light," I told Spike. "Right now we have to check upstairs."

Spike barked repeatedly.

"You're right. We can't watch TV without power." It was 5:55. Instead of checking the rest of the house, I located KTVU on my cell and clicked watch live. Of course, reporters were talking about the earthquake. "We felt our chairs moving beneath our butts," one eyewitness said.

A boy whose voice was changing spoke next. "It sounded like a heavy truck rumbling over rocks. Like four-wheeling."

Then an anchor introduced Tia Wong, who said, "Sixteen-year-old Sandee Mason went through a major scare today. She was perched on top of a ladder, adjusting a stage light in San Ramos High's Little Theatre when the quake erupted. We spoke to her on video chat."

My voice didn't sound like me, and my face looked backwards, but the words were mine. "The ladder was like a roller coaster that had run off the tracks or maybe like riding a surfboard."

"And why were you on top of a ladder?" Ms. Wong asked.

"I'm stage managing *Our Town*, which is San Ramos High's fall play. Ms. G, our teacher, asked me to refocus a light, and one of our stars, Nicole Lorca, was footing the ladder."

"So today's earthquake interrupted your school activities?"

"It interrupted our whole lives."

I was shocked that they cut me off and went to a boy in the parking lot at San Lorenzo High before I even told them the performance dates. Not that it would matter if we couldn't use the theatre. Then I thought about Mrs. Rivera and the images of tipped buildings and jagged sidewalks on the screen. I'd been right when I said it interrupted everything. "How are we going to fix this mess?" I asked Spike.

They interviewed the head of a team inspecting BART and a scratchy-voiced firefighter over in the Fruitvale neighborhood. There was no more news about San Ramos. They didn't even announce which schools were closed.

I texted Jenn, the source of all things gossipy. **You have power? Ours is out.**

Usually she texts right back. There was no light on next door, but I tried Diego anyway. He didn't write back, so I went on to Nicole. Nobody was picking up texts. I didn't have Pete's number in my phone. I didn't even know which apartment he lived in.

My power had dropped to twenty-three percent. Sighing, I stared out the living room window and saw a single, steady beam—not candles or flashlights—coming from across the street. Somebody new now lived in the Bosley family's old place and they had power even though the rest of the block was dark, so I grabbed my laptop and cell, and said, "Watch the house, Spike."

An oppressive stillness bore down on the street. With no headlights or streetlights, my focus sharpened. I pointed my flashlight toward the beam from the window across the street and wished I'd brought my guard dog with me.

Wouldn't the neighbors be safer in their yards? I read Casa Garcia over the mailbox of the Bosley's old place. Mr. Bosley was transferred, and they moved in August so the kids could start the school year in Colorado. We hadn't met the Garcias.

A youngish woman peered through the screen door. She was holding a sleeping baby, and when she saw me reaching for the doorbell she asked, "Can I help you?"

"I'm Sandee Mason from across the street. You have lights."

The woman nodded while her baby burped softly.

"Why? Nobody else has power." She nodded without letting me in. "Do you think maybe I could charge a couple devices? I don't mean to be an imposition, but there's no place else to do it."

She wore capri pants and an Oakland A's shirt splattered in baby dribbles. "Where are you from?" I heard a distinct Hispanic accent.

"Across the street." I pointed to our dark yard. "My dad took off for Cincinnati this morning …" Her forehead scrunched into wrinkles, aging her face. "It's a long story. Nobody has power but you." She looked puzzled, so I slowed down. "You're the only ones in the neighborhood with power. I was on TV tonight, and now I need to charge my devices."

"You were on TV?" she asked.

At the same time a deep voice called, "Who is it, Rosa?"

"Neighbor girl. Wants to charge her devices. Can she use an outlet on your generator?"

"Invite her in. We happily help our neighbors."

The bright kitchen light made me squint.

After Rosa introduced me to her husband, I asked, "How come you have power when no one else does?"

"I brought home a generator." The earth groaned beneath us like a Jeep with no shocks bumping through a dry riverbed. This aftershock rolled more than it erupted. The Garcia's books and breakables stayed on the shelves, and the baby opened his eyes, yawned, and went back to sleep. Would aftershocks be the new normal in California?

"So where were you when the earthquake happened?" I asked Mr. Garcia while plugging my devices into his generator.

"Driving my work truck through Alameda. I could have sworn an ape and a gorilla were jumping on each other in the bed of my pickup."

"What did you do?"

"Pulled over. Got out. Found tools spilled all over and a new shipment of LEDs crushed under a sander. I went by my shop, told the boss, picked up a generator, and brought it home so Rosa could heat the baby's formula."

"Wow! You planned ahead." Everybody had stories about the quake's impact.

He grinned and took the baby from his wife. I was grateful he didn't try to explain generators to me like Dad would have. Instead he said, "So much damage everywhere." Pointing at the TV he asked, "Have you seen the pictures?"

The channel kept replaying the same clip with the same battered Ford Fairlane caught in a gap where a Highway 4 overpass slipped off its pillars, followed by a shot of a car dropping off it and onto I-680. The sky was as light as when the quake first hit. Was traffic still sitting there frozen? The same police officers directed traffic, even though their shifts were probably over by now unless they were rerunning the same clips. Mr. Garcia switched channels and we watched close-ups of a skinny woman pushing a stroller and a man holding two leather briefcases. How had they gotten home?

I no longer wanted to talk about being interviewed. The photos of broken buildings and damaged cars along with the interviews of terrified people seemed much more important than my clinging to a ladder with four people footing it. Who'd clean up the broken concrete?

My phone was charged enough to try Mom again. Dad picked up. "Your mom's sleeping. Traffic is murder. We're spending tonight in Reno, like she told you. Will you be okay if we don't get back until morning?"

"Of course. I can handle it."

"Where are you right now, honey?"

"With the Garcias across the street. He's got a generator."

"You mean there's no power?"

"Nope."

"Okay, we'll get back on the road and try to…"

"Dad, I'm sixteen. I'll be fine."

"Why don't you call Diego's parents? I'm sure you could stay there overnight."

I didn't tell him about the hole in their kitchen or their house being as dark as ours. Instead I asked, "Don't you trust me? Have I ever given you a reason not to?"

"Okay, honey. We'll see you tomorrow. Call anytime you need anything."

"I will." I watched a story about a shop owner in downtown Berkeley giving out water and groceries. He said, "I let people take what they needed, so no one had to steal. I can deduct the missing inventory from my taxes. That's a win-win."

While watching, I typed "Freeway Closures" into Google. A whole string of hits came up, so I tried "Freeway Closures in SF Bay Area today." There were problems on I-680, 580, and 80. The Bay Bridge had shut down. Power blackouts stalled elevators in office buildings and hotels. Electric cars couldn't recharge. Buses needed to be rerouted.

After watching footage of looters fleeing from a computer store in Hayward, I thanked the Garcias, took my laptop and cell, and went home. My footsteps echoed as I crossed the dark street. At least I thought it was my footsteps.

It was way past Spike's dinnertime. I could see his wagging tail in the moonlight. After filling his bowl, I stuck my head out the backdoor, and called, "Spike? Supper!"

He was on the back porch, growling at something. "Spike, it's me. We're the only ones home, but we have flashlights, and everything's charged again."

"Grrrr."

"Maybe we should check upstairs. Flashlight on."

"Flashlight on," Siri answered.

A minute later I heard Spike's toenails clacking against the Pergo floor. He ignored the food while I shined the light up and down the walls. Pictures were crooked, and we saw water spots from the bathroom. Mom would not be pleased. My parents' bedroom looked chaotic; so did mine, but the walls and windows weren't cracked as far as I could see. After a deep breath, I opened the door to Bri's room. A couple of pictures had crashed onto the floor and his bed slid away from the window, showing dust where Mom hadn't swept. As Dad would say, there was no structural damage.

Heading downstairs I asked Spike, "Ready for supper now?"

"Woof!" I clanked a spoon on the edge of his bowl.

"You can eat outside if you want. In fact, I'll join you. That recliner looks pretty inviting, don't you think?" Inside was too quiet. Years ago I learned about staying outside during an earthquake. Spike and I would be fine as long as we stuck together, and the looters stayed away.

I set his bowl on the bricks, and he wolfed his food down. I lay back on the recliner and stared at the night sky. With all the lights out, a million stars danced over me. Spike lay on the grass beside me as if to say, 'You're safe with me, Sandee. I am an outstanding guard dog.'

I glanced at my messages. Nobody called or texted to congratulate me on my TV debut. Not even Diego. Or Pete. Or Nicole. What had happened to the cast of *Our Town*? A gentle breeze ran across my cheeks. They were wet. I wasn't crying, exactly. "What's wrong with me Spike?"

I looked down. He was sleeping. Some watch dog. I just couldn't keep my tears inside and didn't know if I was exhausted, lonely, or scared to death. The wind had blown the haze and pollution away. I stared up at a bevy of stars until sleep took me away.

## Chapter 8

### Friday, October 4, 2017

### Sandee's Home and the Parking Lot in Front of San Ramos High

Aluminum ridges made sharp red marks across my fingers. If gravity sent me plummeting, I'd be a bruised, battered basket case. Below me Tony screamed. Jenn, Nicole, Bradley, Maria, and Ms. G screeched and gasped. I rocked furiously, hurtling toward a giant hole where the floor used to be. Down, down …

My heart thumped into my ribs. I peeled my eyes open, hoping I'd never dream about that moment again. It was worse than my old dreams of Bri burning. I'd been a spectator in those instead of a participant.

Wind whooshed my hair across my cheeks and onto my lips. I'd spent all night in a lounge chair in our back yard. No wonder I shivered so. As the cobwebs cleared, I remembered Mom drove to Reno to bring Dad home because planes couldn't land in Oakland. Flights were cancelled for San Jose, San Francisco, and Sacramento too. Spike and I slept outside. Maybe it was the safest thing to do.

The sky glimmered with early morning light outlining the place where Pine Mountain touched the sky. If this were a scene from *Our Town*, the milkman would be coming around or a kid would be delivering newspapers. Kids on bikes used to deliver newspapers, aiming for the porch with their pitching arm. Now we got our news from TV or online or from social media.

I checked my cell at seven-thirty. Class would start at eight-fifteen. With Dad's car in Oakland, I needed to hurry. After a quick shower, I dressed in low-rise jeans and a forest green tee saying, "We should **all** care." Then I threw on Nikes, slurped some apple juice, and grabbed my backpack.

Oops! Forgot to feed Spike. "If Mom and Dad eat out, they'll bring you leftover bacon," I told him. Diego's house was quiet, so rather than ring the bell, I hurried to school alone, wondering if I could sneak a small cup of Starbucks into first period. By the time I got to Starbucks, kids were already blocking the sidewalks. In first period we'd probably talk about yesterday's earthquake and then write about it, knowing my English teacher. Maybe I could grab a sip of coffee from somebody else—like Diego.

I forgot all about it, though, when I saw students milling around aimlessly, while teachers stood in groups with their school iPads open again. Reams of caution tape closed off every entrance to the school. What was up?

The student council secretary shoved a half page note into my hand.

Because two buildings slipped off their foundations and windows in every wing are broken, the school board recommends that we cancel classes at San Ramos High until professionals assess and correct the situation. We will notify parents by e-mail when we're ready to resume classes.

Tonight's home game has been canceled along with the dance that was to follow. Check the school's website for further updates.

"Hey, Sandee, whatcha doing hanging out here?" Pete stood beside me, leaned against one of the thick metal poles that held up the electric signboard where events were announced.

"I could ask you the same thing."

"I didn't know school was cancelled. You?"

I smiled and shook my head, hoping that just this once my hair bounced like Jenn's.

There was a twinkle in his eye as he said, "Looks like there are a lot of us who didn't know."

The whole situation felt weird and a little wonderful: No classes. No teachers or parents saying what we should do.

"You wanna go somewhere?" Pete asked. My insides tingled. What, exactly, did he have in mind? Was he asking me on a date?

Pete said, "Come on. Where's your car?" I explained about Dad and Reno, and he said, "Do you know when they'll be home?" Again I shook my head. I couldn't talk with my heart in my throat. "Why don't you text them? Say, 'Can they call you when you get to Sacramento?' They'll think you're being responsible, and we'll have plenty of time to get back."

"Back from where?"

"Wherever. Where's your car?"

"I just told you Dad's car is at the airport, and Mom drove hers to Reno to pick him up."

"So let's jump on BART. We could see what's happening over in Hayward."

I shook my head. BART, also known as the Bay Area Rapid Transit system, would have shut down until all the tracks could be checked for earthquake damage. I'd heard about it on the news, and besides I'd seen enough of Hayward last night on Mr. Garcia's TV.

"Why not?" Shrugging, I opened my mouth and closed it again. He waited for a minute while we both watched a crew of seniors pile into their cars and roar off. I thought about Diego and decided his parents got the e-mail.

Pete stood in front of me with his hands in his pockets, grinning. Was his idea scary or awesome?

"I don't think BART's running today."

Pete chuckled. "Don't they put people on buses when the trains aren't running? I mean people have to get from one place to another, right? Come on. Let's go. What have we got to lose?"

He had a point. Who would know? What if I took some amazing photos for Tia Wong and sent them as a follow up on the interview? Maybe the world was giving me a chance to become a more daring young woman.

Always before I'd used school as an excuse to bail me out of uncomfortable situations. I'd say I had to run an errand for Mom or Dad. Or I had rehearsal or homework. Today, though, there was nothing to keep me from going. Besides, he was right. This sounded like a great adventure. So I texted my parents as requested. **Let me know when you get to Sacramento, okay?**

"Good girl," Pete said. "Keeping in touch matters."

I wasn't disobeying any rules. There wasn't school or rehearsal, we weren't having a party, and besides, Mom and Dad liked Pete. They trusted him. Maybe I should too. I thought about a line we'd read in English that said, 'It's easier to ask for forgiveness than permission.' Today it made sense. Pete was so much more mature than Diego, and he wasn't flighty like Jenn. He'd never wind up doing something stupid and messing up his life like Nicole had. Mom and Dad might be proud that I took the initiative to shoot some photos for KTVU.

"We'd better hurry. The bus to BART should be here in about five minutes," I said. He was new and might not even know the bus schedule.

"Perfect. Got any money?" he asked as I took the lead.

Smiling, I held up two twenties and said, "Dad gave me a gas card when I got my license. If we run out of cash, we're still covered."

"Great! Hayward, here we come."

## Chapter 9

### Friday, October 4

### Heading for BART

As we went through the faded orange gates at the BART station, I asked Pete, "Did you text your dad too?"

"Thanks for paying," he said as if he couldn't hear me over the roaring crowd.

P.A. announcements kept saying, "Until the tube has been cleared there is no service into San Francisco. Crews are still repairing the Richmond – Fremont line." The digital signboard added, "Trains run from Antioch to 12$^{th}$ Street only."

"We can't get to Hayward. Shouldn't we do something else?" I shook as an October breeze swept across the platform. Was it from the wind or fear?

"Better get in line," Pete said, as if he hadn't heard me. Too confused to respond, I followed him on a train headed for the MacArthur BART station. It was hard to hear as the train pulled out, so I fiddled with the camera settings on my phone while two women behind us talked about spending last evening in a bar near their office and watching the quake's aftermath on the TV there.

Whenever I ride BART, I usually sit so I can see the crosses on the hill opposite the Lafayette station. There's one representing every soldier who died in Afghanistan. We put up one for Bri in June on the one-year anniversary of his high school graduation. I couldn't spot it from the train since they all look the same—much like soldiers in uniform. The glare made my eyes tear up.

By the time we got to the Orinda stop, I'd grown tired of people talking about fried computer systems, terrified toddlers, and gaping potholes. Only Pete and I found the earthquake's aftermath exhilarating, and I'd started changing my mind. It was one scary mess.

Pete tapped my shoulder, leaned into my ear, and asked, "So if everyone knew a quake would happen on the Hayward Fault, why did people build houses on top of it? And offices?"

"Who knows?" My mouth almost touched his ear. "Dad told me that most people living along the Hayward Fault don't carry earthquake insurance. It's too expensive."

"Bet they're sorry now," he said smiling his know-it-all grin.

"It's kinda sad," I said. Pete either didn't hear me or he ignored me. Sometimes it was hard to tell. He texted, while I stared out the grungy window, hating what he'd said. What was his problem?

We went through the Caldecott Tunnel, which separates Orinda from Berkeley, and slowed down at Rockridge where most commuters were the UC crowd, 20-somethings with backpacks, wheeling their bikes onto BART. The University of California at Berkeley had a station next to the campus, but nobody could use it because it was on the Richmond line. Officials shut it down as soon as the earthquake began, but college students are resilient. Besides AC Transit shuttled people if a station shut down.

The doors closed, and when we got to the MacArthur Station, which was next. Wall-to-wall people jammed into each other. Everybody needed to catch a bus without the Richmond-

Fremont line running. Pete grabbed my hand and said, "Come on."

"Maybe we should turn around," I told Pete as we forced our way into the crowd.

Before we found the line for a bus into Hayward, though, a heavy-set woman in a Transit Authority sweater, whose scalp showed between her cornrows, asked for our IDs.

"Why do you need those?" Pete asked.

"So we can put you on the bus to your neighborhood." Pete looked at me and I looked at him.

As we slipped away, I asked Pete, "Got a Plan B?"

"You watch too many lawyer shows." Why had I come with him?

I started toward the up escalator so we could get back to Walnut Creek. "Wait," Pete shouted. "Do you know that chick waving at us?"

Turning around, I saw Tessa standing by two big cardboard boxes at the gates of the station. I hadn't seen her since I was a guest speaker at a Gold Star event she hosted in Berkeley last August. She and her mom are active in Gold Star and Blue Star, and I met them at a meeting last spring right before we learned that an IED blew Bri into a million pieces.

I grabbed Pete's hand and together we pushed our way through businesspeople with laptops, students with backpacks, and shoppers carrying grocery bags. After Tessa finished giving a receipt to an older woman, I said, "Hey, stranger, how've you been?"

"Sandee, hi. Who's this guy?"

"Pete. Pete Benson, this is Tessa Kwan. She did the set decorations for *Oklahoma* before she graduated last spring!"

They said hello and I asked, "How's your sister?"

"She can wiggle her fingers and toes now." Tessa's older sister had been in the Army at the same time Bri was. We both wondered if their paths ever crossed. She came back from Afghanistan in a coma instead of a body bag, and sometimes I wondered which one was harder on the families and friends left behind.

"Has she said anything?"

Tessa shook her head. "The doctors say there's movement behind her eyelids. That's all they can tell us."

I hated how the wars in Afghanistan, Syria, and Iraq tore people apart. Sometimes I hated Bri for going. When I told Tessa, she explained I was confusing hate with loneliness, which helped me rethink things. There were so many battles in the world—including battles with nature—like the earthquakes and winds the environment kept throwing at us. Maybe the battle with global warming had gotten closer than ever. Bad enough that we'd been having fires every October for years. I didn't want to think such serious thoughts, so I asked, "What are you collecting?"

"Clothes for people who've been relocated to shelters. It's not like they can go home and pack a bag if their houses are red-tagged."

"Pretty quick for the Blue Star Moms to get organized, isn't it?" Their literature sat on a card table between the two boxes of clothing.

"I take those everywhere, Sandee. Sometimes I pass them out at school because you never know, but I'm collecting this for the Red Cross."

"Where do you find the time?" Before she could answer, a couple of UC Berkeley students dragged a garbage bag full of clothes toward her.

The blonde said, "These are from all the women in Sigma

Chi. Everybody's getting involved and we wanted to contribute what we could." Both girls were dressed in black leggings. One wore a blue and gold UC Berkeley tee while the other was in an oversized Zeta Psi shirt with the American names spelled out under the Greek letters that identified the fraternity.

"Someday you're going to start your own non-profit, aren't you?" I said after the sorority girls took their receipt and waltzed off.

"Great idea! Maybe I'll open a gallery. Except a gallery shouldn't be a non-profit. Artists have as much right to earn money as anyone."

"Right." Tessa had great ideas, and I loved the way she put them into action.

"If you or your family have any clothes to donate… and that goes for you too," she said turning to Pete. "Got anything to donate?"

He shook his head and said, "Our clothes are still in transit, but what you're doing is wonderful."

"If Mom or Dad have stuff, I'll text you," I said. "We can deliver it after my parents get back from Reno."

"Reno?"

Our conversation stopped while Tessa accepted a donation from an elderly man carrying a stack of baseball caps and packages of socks with the cardboard wrapping still around them.

"Betcha they're stolen," Pete whispered.

"And you know this because…?"

His eyes twinkled as he said, "Because I watch all the detective shows instead of lawyer shows."

"Sandee, I'm surprised your parents didn't come back as soon as they heard about the quake," Tessa said.

Pete's phone buzzed, and he said, "Be right back. Wait here."

"He's hot, but how do you put up with his telling you what to do?" Tessa asked as soon as he was out of earshot.

"We're not a couple." Cute as he was, he'd just given me an order instead of asking a question. Not good—not for a boyfriend or a platonic friend.

Switching subjects, I told Tessa about Dad's flight and the return trip being rerouted and school closing while they cleaned up. She nodded and her eyes filled with concern. By the time I was done, there were people waiting in line to donate and Pete was back with a grin on his face and a hungry glow in his eye. "Let her collect, Sandee. We need to go."

"Go where?" I asked as we walked away. "We can't get to Hayward."

"We could use Uber. Got an account?

"No," I said in the are-you-kidding-me tone that makes Dad think I need to show more respect. It went right over Pete's head.

"Wanna go downtown? Nineteenth Street and Twelfth Street are the next two exits."

"Why go into Oakland?"

"To people watch. They won't ask for IDs for that."

Someone with spray paint had scrawled "Tectonic Time Bomb Explodes" along the cement edge of the platform. "Why would anyone risk their lives to post graffiti?" I asked to change the subject.

I was surprised when Pete said, "Probably a dare. Frat guys do that to each other all the time. Let's get back on BART. Riding around is way better than hanging out in San Ramos."

"Going downtown won't give me the photos I'm looking for. Don't you think we should…?" My phone buzzed. A text from Mom said, We're at the south end of Sacramento. Traffic is mostly going the other way now. See you soon.

"We're going home, Pete. Mom and Dad are about an hour away." I started back upstairs but Pete grabbed the waistband of my jeans. "What are you doing?"

"Encouraging you to stay. Your parents like me, remember?"

"If you want me to like you, *let go*. I'm going home. If you want to stay, that's fine."

Being here, surrounded by crowds pushing their way home made me jittery. Those horrible moments when I was swaying on top of the ladder ran through my mind again. I'd never felt so nervous in a crowd, and I wasn't sure if this was related to my ladder moment, but maybe the aluminum monstrosity incident scared me worse than I thought. The world had turned crazy and I craved something familiar. Pete had been filling the bill, right up to the moment where he grabbed me.

Abruptly, he said, "You're right. Your parents are almost home. I'll get you back so they never need to know."

I looked him straight in the eye, and said, "You don't have to take me anywhere." Our gazes locked until he broke into a smile. "You're pretty cool. Most girls would have caved and gone to Oakland with me."

"Silly boy. I'm not most girls."

He gave me an amazing smile. "I'm kinda figuring that out."

# Chapter 10

## Friday, October 4, 2017

### Back Home

I silently asked Bri what the consequences of this earthquake would be. No way I'd ask Bri anything out loud with Pete listening. Pete didn't know anything about Bri's messages, and I couldn't risk his hearing me over the train's chugging. After a minute I realized Bri had nothing to say to me. No surprise. His silence meant I was doing fine, and maybe he approved of Pete.

I felt good while we waited for the bus from the Walnut Creek Station to San Ramos. No one knew we weren't a couple. Staring out another grubby window once we got on the 331 bus, I saw that the trees were still rooted in the ground, though more branches than usual were blowing around like rubbish. Leaves scattered as our bus whooshed by. No gaping holes tried to swallow the bus, and the homes we passed looked secure. The crooked fence and bent driveway gate could have happened before the quake. Maybe the homeowners needed an insurance payout before they could get it repaired. We had no reason to blame it on the earthquake.

The bus stopped in front of the high school, and I stood up. "Coming?" I asked when Pete didn't move.

He shook his head. "I'm meeting a friend." The sun cast wavy shadows as I walked home. Halfway there, I realized it made no sense for Pete to ask me to hang out in Oakland if he was meeting a friend here. Maybe he got a text while I daydreamed about Bri and the earthquake disaster? But wouldn't I have noticed?

As I walked toward home, I saw two little girls in matching pigtails playing hopscotch, a man wheeling his garbage can to the curb, and a U-Haul van in front of Diego's house. Was somebody—maybe a family from Hayward or San Leandro—moving in with the Riveras? Would their house be big enough? Did they have a daughter who would steal Diego's heart? Not that it would be stealing since it never belonged to me.

Since Mom's car wasn't in the driveway yet, I knocked on his door. Instead of letting me in, Diego shushed me, and I wondered what the big secret was as he walked me to the striped canvas swing on their brick porch. Before I could ask what was going on, he said, "We're moving away. We'll be at my aunt's house."

"Which aunt?"

"Mom's sister. She lives in a godforsaken place called Fallon, Nevada."

My heart dropped. "How far away is that?"

"Halfway to Utah. There's nothing there."

"Not even a school?"

"Moron," he snarled.

"Toad," I shot back.

"Dweeb!" We called each other those names in seventh grade. Now we laughed at ourselves until his eyes filled again. "Mom's too freaked to stay here, and she wants to be with her sister. They fought PTSD together in Mexico City. Besides, a gas pipe under Dad's restaurant exploded last night and the place…went up in…flames."

"OMG! Are you making this up?"

"I wish. The kitchen, the bar, and most of the chairs and tables are gone. There's burned timber and ashes all over, and the police cordoned off the whole block. Dad said the owner told him the building's a total loss. His voice trembled. "Will you watch out for Maria?"

"Can you at least come back and see her in *Our Town*?"

He shrugged because he didn't know if he could come any more than I knew if there'd be a play. Stuff was closing down everywhere—damaged places like schools and stores, dangerous places like freeway overpasses, and places we hadn't even heard about. Marvin's, where we hung out after performances, was closed for repairs, and there was caution tape around the playgrounds in all the parks. How were we supposed to cope with no place to go, nothing to do, and no way to stop the vibrating aftershocks?

There was still texting, music, and TikTok, but that wasn't enough to fill the whole day. No school meant no play, no responsibilities, and no homework. I used to think that would be great, but the reality felt hollow. With the holidays coming and finals in January, there wouldn't be two weekends together when we could perform until sometime in February. By then we were usually hard at work on the musical.

Our whole year was ruined, and we were only in October. If there was no play, I couldn't be the stage manager any more. I'd only be a girl with a bad algebra grade, whose best friend moved to Fallon, where he'd be surrounded by sagebrush, cactus, and girls I didn't know. "What am I going to do when you aren't next door?"

Instead of answering, he pointed to my house. Mom's car was pulling into our driveway. Dad's car was probably stuck in

Oakland. I had no idea how we'd get it home with all the freeway closures.

I reached for Diego's hand, which felt as icy as Lake Tahoe in winter. "You scared?"

"Kinda. Mostly sad."

"We'll still text and call."

"It's not the same."

Slowly I nodded, thinking of the burned-out restaurant and our closed high school. "Nothing's going to be the same for a long time. When do you leave?"

"I dunno. Mom wants to leave today, but Dad said I need to help him close the house and pack the U-Haul first."

I wanted to kiss him so badly, but when I leaned toward him, he turned away.

"Your parents are waving," he said.

I turned and waved back. "Be right there," I called across the remains of Mom's camellia bushes. Then I turned back to Diego and took his hand in mine. "Come say good-bye before you go, okay?"

"If you hear the U-Haul starting, you come over and say good-bye," he answered.

"I love you," I whispered.

All he could do was nod. Those words were too hard for him.

I went through the gate that separated our two yards and threw my arms around Dad. I was so grateful we weren't running away to live with some aunt in Nevada. "Where were you when you heard the news?"

"Cleveland Airport. I never got to the conference."

"But weren't they giving you an award?"

"They can mail it to me. At a time like this, it's more important to be available for my family and my clients." We were already in the house when he asked, "Why is there a U-Haul at the Rivera's place?"

"It's so awful, Dad. A gas leak caused a fire that ruined their restaurant, and his mom's freaking out 'cause their chimney and kitchen are falling apart and she never got over the Mexico City quake."

"What does that have to do with a U-Haul truck?"

"They're going to live with his aunt in the middle of Nevada."

"I never saw that woman afraid of anything," Mom said, shaking her head as she dropped her purse on the table by the door. I knew she meant Mrs. Rivera. Mom was right. Scary how quickly she became unhinged.

After going upstairs, Dad put the suitcase on the bed, Mom opened it, and the two of them unpacked it together. Sometimes it's fun to watch them get all absorbed in each other.

As I watched them unpacking, I remembered that Tessa needed clothes. Since Dad had been going to a conference, he'd packed his good suit. I knew he wouldn't want to give that away, but I still asked, "Either of you have any old clothes you want to donate to people whose homes were destroyed?"

They both stared like I'd gone nuts. "Why are you asking?" Mom finally said.

"You remember Tessa?"

Mom nodded. Dad folded his arms.

"She's collecting stuff for people who had to ... you know ... evacuate. People who left with no clothes, because they only had five minutes. People whose houses are red tagged."

They looked at each other before Mom said, "When did you run into Tessa?"

"Earlier today. Why?"

"Where have you been, Sandee?" Dad asked. He sounded more curious than mad, but if I didn't come up with a good answer, I'd be toast.

"Well…the school texted you, right?"

Dad turned to Mom. "I didn't get a text. Did you?"

"No."

"I guess there was some kind of glitch. Lots of families didn't get them so a bunch of us showed up at school. Classes were cancelled. Nobody can get into the science and art wings."

"Why?" Dad asked.

"Because of the earthquake. Two wings slid off their foundations. I guess they needed time to figure out where to put those classes. I've got a paper telling all about it." I began digging in my backpack.

"But Tessa attends Pine Mountain College up in Pleasant Hill, and I imagine she lives around there now. What were you doing in Pleasant Hill?" Mom said.

"Nothing." Mom's eyebrows shot up. "The last time I went up there we were on a drama field trip, remember?" She could tell I was avoiding the truth. Should I tell them I let Pete talk me into a trip on BART, pretend I went alone, or just change the subject as soon as possible? They didn't understand how cool Pete was. He'd taken me on an adventure, but I didn't know how to explain it. They still expected me to ask for permission before I went anywhere.

"Did she call you asking for donations?" Mom asked. When I said nothing, she added, "May I see your phone?"

"I erased the call."

Dad tapped his foot repeatedly, which meant he was running out of patience. "The truth, please."

"Promise you won't get mad." The air was thick with their

silence. No way I'd let them treat me the way Nicole's parents treated her. How I wished Pete had stuck around so he could help me explain.

"Since there was no school, I was going to come home, even though nobody was here, but I ran into Pete in the parking lot. You remember him?" They both nodded, while Mom zipped the suitcase. Dad stood with his arms still folded, waiting. "Pete said maybe we could get pictures of the epicenter in Hayward for the TV stations. Wouldn't that be a great thank you for their interview yesterday?"

Dad's arms were still folded. Mom now sat with her head in her hands.

"I told Pete the trains to Hayward would be stopped until they checked the tracks, but he told me they'd have buses. So once we got to the MacArthur Station, I saw Tessa collecting clothing for people who'd been displaced. Everybody was donating. Isn't that awesome?"

"What if you weren't here when we got home?" Dad asked. His chin trembled the way it does when he gets upset.

"You would have called me, and I would have said where I was. Maybe you would have been proud of me for taking care of myself so well."

Mom's worry wrinkles were deeper than ever. "Young lady, do you think it's wise to risk being caught in an aftershock while you're on a train that could derail?"

"What were you thinking, taking a seat when so many people don't have any other way to get home from work?" Dad added.

"And why were you leaving town without letting anyone know when we should expect you back?" Mom asked.

"But none of that happened."

Dad said, "You don't realize that it could have. Do you have any idea how much loss has resulted from that quake?"

"Sure. The school's shut down, rehearsals are cancelled, and if we can't get back soon, Nicole won't get her credits and graduate in January."

Dad shook his head, and I knew I'd said the wrong thing. "You and I are going for a drive tomorrow morning. Bring your friend Pete if you want to. I'll show you some devastation you can't even imagine. I've had calls from sixty-seven people with claims of property damage and loss. After you see the damage, you'll understand how serious this is. It might make you see why your decision was wrong."

"I can bring Pete?" Maybe I should ask if I could bring Diego instead, but he would be packing the U-Haul. Besides, he hadn't done anything wrong. I didn't really think we had either, but maybe I'd understand Pete better if I spent a little more time with him.

He nodded. "I don't know what his parents were thinking about, but you kids need to realize how widespread the destruction is."

That's when I remembered that I never even saw Pete text his parents. He had so much more freedom than I did.

## Chapter 11

### Saturday, October 5

### San Ramos

As I opened my eyes the next morning, I remembered my message telling Pete he could join Dad and me on some insurance calls. He hadn't answered, so I left him another text—so he wouldn't miss out.

While I was checking them, I found one from Jenn written the day before: More broken glass all over campus. Dr. Henderson said GO HOME. Looks like a bomb exploded.

There was a longer text from Ms. G to the whole cast saying, The impact of the earthquake is beyond our control. Practice your lines. Consider objectives and relationships. Work on scenes with each other if you can get together. When I know more, I'll share it.

So *Our Town* wasn't canceled...but it wasn't scheduled either. Ms. G wanted us to rehearse, and our house would be a great place to do it. But if Dad was taking me on his insurance calls, how could I invite cast members over?

I admit I was curious to see if the disasters lived up to the complaints people phoned in and how people reacted under stress like this. Maybe it's the drama geek in me.

The principal wouldn't let kids on campus, as Jenn made abundantly clear, but I could do other things, like take some local pictures instead of ones from Hayward. Maybe the news tip lines would be interested, and I'd get a photo credit. Maybe our journalism class would put them on the school website.

Dad spoke through my closed bedroom door. "We'll be starting at my office this morning. Get your stuff and…"

"But…"

"Please don't interrupt, Sandee. Bring your backpack and your phone and be in the car in three minutes." I heard his footsteps as he walked down the hall. He meant business. Silently I sat in the back seat of Mom's car. We dropped her at Alicia's Antiques and headed for Dad's office. Neither of us said a word until we got there and he gave me my orders. "I expect you to listen to the messages on the recorder and forward whatever's urgent to my personal line. You're a good organizer, right?"

"Right."

"Excellent. This is important and hearing the voices of devastated people will give you a whole new perspective."

I sat at his secretary's desk, and he pointed at the blinking light flashing the number eighty-three over and over. "Eighty-three calls in two days?"

"Exactly. People who can't afford earthquake insurance often look for compensation from their homeowner's policy. Urgent calls are from people with medical issues or earthquake insurance. Forward them. For the rest, give me their name, phone number, and problem as succinctly as possible. Handle these as quickly as you can because they keep pouring in and leave the drama out of it."

"But I've never … How do I?"

"You know how-to pick-up messages, Sandee. You do it all the time. I'll be in my office."

At least Pete wasn't stuck with this task. He would have hated it. Hours later, when I looked out the window, the sun was sinking beneath the ridge. The whole day disappeared while I processed messages. I'd missed lunch and only handled fifty-six calls. Another sixteen came in while I worked. All day I heard "cracked sidewalk," "wind damage," "leaky pipes," "broken glass," "missing shingles," and "cracked dishes." Amy Brenner had been hospitalized after her car went off the road. Jimmy Whelan stumbled over a jagged sidewalk, tripped, and broke his ankle. "Shouldn't Amy Brenner and Jimmy Whelan talk to whoever carries their medical insurance?" I asked Dad when he came out of his office for another cup of coffee.

"People pay for insurance their whole life. When they have a claim, they want all the money they're entitled to. My job is to make sure they're taken care of while protecting our home office."

"I thought you sold insurance."

"I do. That means I'm the one they know. If a claim sounds valid, I'll tell them how to file it with an adjuster. If their insurance won't cover it, I have to tell them that. Aren't you glad I'm not asking you to call those people?"

"Yes, but you told me earthquake insurance is so expensive people can't afford it."

"Even if I can't validate a claim, I can help a family locate a missing cat or refer them to someone who patches walls. Come on now. We've already got five places to visit tomorrow."

"On Sunday?"

"Crises operate 24-7." Stuffing a bunch of papers in his briefcase he added, "Would you like to drive home?"

"Sure." He tossed me Mom's keys. Maybe this wouldn't be so bad after all. Because I was driving, my cell stayed in my backpack, so I didn't find Nicole's text until I pulled out my cell after dinner. **Can you help me with lines for Act III? Maybe come over?**

I clicked on her number.

Her phone only rang once. "I'm so glad you called. We've got aftershocks running under the house. Do you feel them where you are?"

"No. I'm in my room upstairs." I looked around. A couple of books had tipped over, but they stayed in the bookcase. My lipstick and mascara were on their sides beneath my dressing table, but they were little. We didn't have gaps in the wall like Diego's kitchen.

"I don't know what to do," Nicole continued. "I'm alone, and it's not like we have a dog."

"You're right! Spike predicts aftershocks. I'll ask Dad if I can bring our personal earthquake detective over."

Nicole envied my freedom, so I wasn't surprised when she said, "You have to ask your parents?" After I explained about my BART trip with Pete, she said, "They should let you grow up. I'd feel a whole lot safer with you and Spike here. Tell your dad you'd be helping a friend."

"Good plan. Be there in fifteen minutes." I got Spike's leash and told Dad, "Nicole's feeling aftershocks that we're not getting here, so she asked if I could bring Spike over. You know he has his own, built-in, early warning system."

Dad sounded surprised as he said, "I taught you that. Don't stay out too late, and bring the car back with a full tank." I was surprised and relieved that he let me go. Maybe Mom told him he'd overreacted, or maybe a client said something that changed his mind.

"And remember to slide the driver's seat back where you found it." It was such a routine request that he didn't even look up.

Fifteen minutes later I rang Nicole's doorbell. Spike's tongue hung out of his mouth as he panted over nothing, which was his way of saying that everything was normal.

Nicole answered the door with her script in hand. "Come on in, you guys. Spike sniffed every wall and baseboard, as he does in each new room, checking out the floorboards and indoor plants with amazing intensity. "Want Coke or water?" she asked.

"Water would be good. Thanks."

The minute she walked out of the kitchen, water bottles in hand, Spike started growling, scratching, and running from one end of the room to the other. He headed for the door we'd just come in. Nicole's eyes widened. "It's happening again, and he knows it, right?"

"Exactly," I said, putting his leash back on. "Are we safe in here?"

"Who knows? Aren't we supposed to get under a doorframe whenever there's an aftershock?"

"Right." We both stared at each other. I pointed at the kitchen door, and we got there at the same time.

"Can you ask Siri what's going on?"

"Siri," I said, while holding Spike's leash, "why are there earthquake swarms in Sycamore Heights?"

Siri listed websites about recent earthquake swarms. Rocks and fissures moving underground had stirred up faults throughout the state. I imagined underground caves and stalactites, damp and slimy. Each shift bumped another fault into action and the quakes were coming from the San Andreas and Calaveras Faults as well as Hayward, which wasn't normal.

If different tectonic plates shifted all at once, were we ramping up for a war with our own planet? Were there faults we knew nothing about? Would we put bridges over the gaping holes in roads? And why were we feeling so much in Sycamore Heights? Artificial intelligence can only share facts already in print. Reasoning requires human brains.

None of this explained why Nicole's house had earthquakes and ours didn't. To relax her I only said, "I think it's too soon for Google or Siri to know. Somebody has to program this stuff and it's too soon for that."

Before she could answer, Spike woofed up another storm and ran across the room from corner to corner, dodging the heavy coffee table and the furniture filling the floor. He barked like squirrels and raccoons were attacking through every door and window. A minute later the house rocked, back and forth—thud, thud. The lights flashed twice, and we were plummeted into darkness.

Nicole asked, "Why is this happening to us?" in a frail, fearful voice that made her sound about twelve. "What's going on?"

Her rising panic scared me. My hands shook, so it took me three tries to get my cell phone flashlight turned on. While I was struggling with it, I remembered the disturbances in *Poltergeist*. Sure it's a movie, but sometimes real life is stranger than fiction. Imagining disaster scenes was not a good coping strategy.

"I can't stand being alone when everything's out. The DVR. The digital clocks. The hanging lamp by the patio door that stays on all the time. This is freaking me out."

"Me too. Where do you Lorcas keep your flashlights?" My voice stayed steady as I spoke.

"There's one in the hutch by the front door."

"Excellent. Spike. Front door." Spike, who had been hunkering by my feet waiting for the next aftershock, leapt up and bounced across the floor.

"Wow. When he moves his collar lights up. He's quite the dog."

"Absolutely! Good boy, Spike." Nicole rummaged around, pulled out a slim object, hit a button, and a dim beam wavered.

"Got any batteries?"

"I don't know."

She sounded like my mom did when she was shutting down, so I asked, "What's really going on?"

"What do you think's going on? Our world is falling apart!"

"Maybe, but it hasn't happened yet, and it's not like we have a way to fix earthquakes. We needed a distraction."

"I need to know where my parents are."

"What?"

"You might as well know, Sandee. You're more level-headed than most of the people in this town. Mom's at the store, trying to pretend everything's normal, but it's not. We haven't heard from my dad since the earthquake, and my mom keeps saying he'll be back any time. I cannot live with all her denial!"

"O.M.G! Nicole, I had no idea. Where was he when the big one hit?"

She shook her head. "His office is in Emeryville, but he could have been out on a sales call. He could have been in Berkeley or Palo Alto or anywhere in the Bay Area."

"The police are looking for him, right?"

How many others were they looking for too, I wondered as she said, "They better be. Mom thinks she's protecting me by keeping her mouth shut, but I can't stand not knowing. In rehab they teach you about the importance of total honesty, and Mom knows that, but she can't even be honest with herself. I'd cope with the power outage if I weren't terrified that Dad fell into some sinkhole, and nobody's looking for him. Every aftershock makes me afraid he's getting buried deeper."

More of her living room had plunged into darkness. "Can you check with the police?"

"I don't know the case number, and Mom's probably told them not to talk to me. She still thinks I'll drink again if anything bad happens, and she doesn't have a clue that she's the one who's stressing me out. Last time I asked her what she was hiding, she sent me on an errand to stop the conversation."

"How can I help?"

She sat for a moment, staring into her lap, before she said, "Do you think I could spend the night at your house?"

"Great idea. Let me call my parents while you text your mom. And don't ask for permission. Tell her you're coming with me and you'll be safe."

If my dad disappeared… I couldn't finish my thought. Not after we lost Bri. We needed Dad, Nicole needed her dad, and I'd find a way to help her locate him. But how?

As we headed for the car, I felt like Bri was high-fiving me. Okay, I felt a warm glow—like a blanket of hope wrapping around me. Could he see Nicole's father even though we couldn't?

## Chapter 12

### Sunday, October 6

### Driving in the East Bay

The next morning, instead of going back to work with Dad, Nicole and I headed for her dad's office in Emeryville. Mom loaned me her car with a lot of warnings about being careful, since Dad's car was still in long-term parking. I checked Google for road closures, but there were no new problems, which was a relief.

Despite the importance of this trip, my mind wasn't on Nicole or her dad as we left San Ramos. I couldn't stop thinking about saying good-bye to Diego earlier. He'd texted me at seven-thirty, and I sneaked out and met him by the U-Haul. His mom was already in the passenger seat with her arms folded, and his dad was double-checking to make sure the kitchen was blocked off with plywood, tarps, and wire. Diego's uncle said he'd find a repairman who could get the kitchen shored up within the week, and he promised to check the place every day. Then the two brothers hugged.

The world was so still that I almost believed the earthquake never happened. "We're going to stay in touch, right?" I asked Diego.

"Yup," he said, patting the cell in his pocket.

"And we're going to see each other again?"

"I want to see Maria perform and check in with the band. God, I'm going to miss the band, but we have to go." For a moment neither of said a word. We simply stood there, drinking in the morning sunshine and wishing we could stay together. At least that's what I wished. He surprised me when he added, "I'm not afraid of starting over."

He choked on the last words and turned away, but I put my arms around him and held on tight. "I love you, you know."

"Love you too," he whispered. Always before the words had been too hard for him to say.

I stood with Maria and her family as Mr. Rivera backed out of the driveway, and I was still there after everyone else had gone back home. What was I going to do without Diego? Who was going to make me laugh?

"You're awfully quiet this morning," Nicole said as we got on the freeway later. "Is everything okay?"

"Just thinking about Diego leaving."

"You two weren't like all the official couples," she said. "You really cared about each other."

Her words filled my heart. She thought we were a couple. "We still care, and he's coming back to see Maria in *Our Town*, assuming we find a place to rehearse and perform."

"The school's still standing, and I'll bet a broom is all they need to make the Little Theatre safe."

"Have you been inside?" I asked even though students weren't allowed on campus.

"No. It's common sense—or maybe an instinct. We'll get to do the show." I knew she was trying to make me feel better, but there was a hole in my heart without Diego, and I didn't know how anyone could fill it. He was the one I always turned to. I couldn't get him out of my mind. "Want to stop for donuts? My treat."

That was just as odd as Dad letting me take her to

Emeryville. When we were doing *Oklahoma!* Nicole talked to me about how much sugar I ate and how it was every bit as addictive as alcohol. Now she was offering to feed that addiction. Unless she thought it was no longer a daily habit and an occasional treat wouldn't hurt. Maybe sugar wasn't as addictive as alcohol. I hadn't seen her consume anything stronger than the coffee she had in her commuter cup. Ever. I couldn't help wondering what she was like when she drank. "You know how I love glazed old-fashioned donuts."

"How about one of those for you and a plain one for me?"

"That'd be great." One was better for me than two, and I'd already eaten a bowl of cereal before I dashed out of the house.

"Just one thing. Can they wait until after we check my dad's office? We're almost there."

"Of course," I said imagining the donut's slick glaze melting in my mouth and tingling my tongue.

When we pulled into the parking lot of the office complex where Mr. Lorca worked, we gasped simultaneously. The building itself was cock-eyed and splitting apart at the seams. Steel and glass hung askew. At least a quarter of it had sunk into the cement, which meant the foundation cracked, split and slid into the earth. Little hills and valleys ruptured the parking lot's surface. I didn't know where to put the car or how we were going to get through the door that had jammed itself into the cement.

A man in a rent-a-cop uniform rushed up to us. "You can't drive around in here. Only emergency personnel are allowed."

Nicole leaned across and said, "This is an emergency. My father works here and no one has heard from him since the quake hit."

"Personnel have all been cleared. You can't stay here."

"But…"

He put a hand on the pistol in his holster. Did he think we were looters or was trespassing enough to shoot people now?

"Okay," I said and turned so fast the tires squealed. Out on the street I asked, "What now?"

Nicole pressed her fingertips against her temples, which reminded me of my headaches right after the earthquake. "Beats me." Her voice quaked. "I'm not even sure he went to the office that day. Sometimes he makes presentations or talks to clients in their offices, so he might not have been here."

"His car's not in your garage, is it?"

"Duh, Sandee. No way."

"Sorry." I couldn't think clearly. "This place has been evacuated, and he hasn't called. That's what's so scary. Could he have lost his phone?"

"Responsible grown-ups don't lose their phones. Besides, he'd have borrowed one." We were already on San Pablo Avenue, but I had no idea where we should go next, so I pulled over to the curb as soon as I saw a legitimate parking space. "Would your mom know where he was headed on Thursday?"

Nicole stared at her hands as she said, "Umm...I don't want to disturb her."

I hated her relationship with her mom, but I only said, "You don't have a choice. Your dad's missing, and we have to find him. We don't even know if your mom reported it. That's what mine would have done." A police car slowed as it passed us. "Call your mom and ask her to look on his calendar. Or the family calendar. Do you have one of those?" I asked.

"Of course. Heaven forbid we should bend a rule," she said as she texted her mom. The school district recommended their family calendars as a way to keep track of activities and assignments. It was great if your kids still needed rides but a little silly if you had a license.

"I guess we go back?" I asked, turning the engine back on.

Nicole nodded and I took the San Pablo Dam Road exit, which would take us over to Highway 24. "At least we know two places where he isn't." She didn't say anything.

The older houses we passed were sloped at odd angles. Of course they didn't have seven floors, like the office building where Nicole's dad worked. They weren't shiny or new, and if these people didn't have earthquake insurance... OMG. Dad was rubbing off on me.

We passed a bunch of middle school kids on bikes looking for damage to explore. "At least if your mom is taking care of your brothers, you don't have to babysit." She was slumped in her seat, staring at nothing. To pull her out of her funk I said, "Hey, want to stop at the next shopping center? There's a donut shop there."

"Why not?" she said and tucked her phone in its pocket. "Can I ask you something, Sandee?"

"Sure."

"How did you get that reporter from KTVU to put your earthquake story on the air?"

My eyes widened. "I didn't know anybody saw it."

"Jenn texted the whole cast five minutes before you were on. You were pretty impressive. A little hyper maybe, but you sounded authentic, and I knew it was true because I was a part of it."

"I had no idea anybody saw it. Getting interviewed is really easy. Just Google the TV channels and the radio stations in the East Bay and search for 'tip lines.' The more requests you send, the better your chances of getting called. Tia Wong said I had a great human-interest story, and I'm sure yours is too." Silently she started texting or researching. I couldn't tell which, but I had to ask one more thing. "Why hasn't anybody said they saw me on TV?"

"I just did. Diego was probably packing up his family's stuff, or he would have said something." I remembered the power failure on our street that night. He wasn't on the cast list, or he would have called. Now I couldn't even ask if he'd seen me. "And you know how Bradley and Amber can be. If it's not about them…" Amber played Emily Webb, next door neighbor of George Gibb, which was Bradley's role. "Well, anyway," Nicole continued, "most kids are probably just jealous because you were really good."

I swung into the lot, parked, and we walked into the donut shop together. "One glazed old-fashioned, right?"

"Yup."

"Coffee or tea?"

"Tea."

We sat across from each other at a red Formica table that looked vintage. I'd started eating before she asked, "Do you think you could maybe get Tia Wong to talk to me?"

"I can try. You want to ask people to look for your father?"

"Of course. There are posters of missing people all over the place. We need more than that," she said, fingering her donut without eating it.

"I'd love to help you, but I have to ask you something she's going to ask. Why should she pick your story?" I bit off another chunk of the sugary goodness and rolled it around my tongue while she answered.

"Maybe I'm not all that special, but my dad is. I know that's no reason, but maybe he could be some kind of a symbol of all the people who are missing?"

I nodded and said, "Say that again with confidence." She giggled, because I was falling into the role of director again, but she did as I said—with conviction. Right then and there, I scrolled through my phone, found Tia Wong's number, and listened to her say, "I want to hear your story. Please leave a message with a contact number, and I'll get back to you as soon as I can."

I handed Nicole my phone saying, "Leave your message," and she did. She sounded a little like her Stage Manager character, who is incredibly confident.

When she handed the phone back to me, I said, "My turn to ask another question. Do you ever hear from Rob any more?"

She almost did a spit take. Rob was Nicole's boyfriend when she was drinking. He was a couple of years older than me, and I knew him first as Bri's best friend and later as the stage manager of *Oklahoma!* The day before we opened, he got arrested for being under the influence. That's how I got to be stage manager right before we opened. Rob got sent to rehab, which he deserved, but I always felt bad that I got to be stage manager because he messed up. This time, though, I'd earned the job.

"Rob got his GED because he didn't want to come back to San Ramos High. I heard that he got a job in a movie theatre up in Pleasant Hill. Can you see him picking up garbage after the movie ends?"

"No way."

"I don't know if he'll stay sober or not," Nicole continued. "He called me in September to find out if I wanted to take the GED with him. I said no, and I haven't heard from him since."

"Do you miss him?" I asked, thinking about Diego.

She shook her head. "Being his girlfriend was stupid. I thought he knew everything when we first met, but all he knew how to do was push people into risky stuff they didn't want to do."

"Sad case," I said as we got back on the road. The trees thickened as they always did right before the reservoir. Looking over, we both saw waves sparkling, and I wondered if any of the cement that kept the water in the dam had cracked. We didn't need another disaster.

Walking into her house, she said, "Let's check the calendar." Sure enough, her father had penciled in an appointment at the bookstore on the UC campus for Thursday morning. We were looking in the wrong place. "Can you use people locator on your phone?"

She sighed. "Dad can track me, but it's not set up to work both ways. I'm going to try the number he left on the calendar and see if it still works."

## Chapter 13

### Sunday, October 6

### Nicole's House

"They're not open," Nicole said as I sipped the cup of tea she brought me after taking the phone number of the UC Berkeley Bookstore off the family calendar. "They're transferring me to the UC switchboard."

"Maybe he was trying to sell them a new media campaign?" I asked.

She sighed. "That's beside the point. Where is he now?"

The back door burst open and her younger brother announced, "Mama says we have to be quiet cause she has a headache." His older brother chased him through the kitchen and into the living room.

"Hello, girls. Did you discover anything in Emeryville?" Mrs. Lorca asked.

"He wasn't there. He had an appointment at the UC Bookstore," Nicole said. Mrs. Lorca started pulling cans out of the grocery bags. "Did you hear me, Mom?"

After a deep sigh, she said, "You're a better detective than I thought. I didn't want to worry you, and I figured if you had something to do, you'd feel like you were helping."

Honestly, parents shouldn't have kids if they're not going to trust them.

I looked at Nicole and she looked at me. Then she told her

mom exactly what she should have said months ago. "Mom, it's time to trust me again. I know I made a big mistake, but that's in the past. I'm doing everything the court said I had to, and I'm helping you, but you need to realize I'm old enough to move out if I decide to."

Mrs. Lorca turned away from the bag she was emptying and faced us. "I suppose that's true, but I didn't want to worry you."

"Oh, Mom, isn't that what family is for? I don't want to desert you, but I will if you can't stop treating me like a fragile child."

"I'm not…"

"Yes, you are. Sandee spent all morning driving me around when you knew we wouldn't find anything. Please tell us what you know."

"All right, since you asked, that morning he texted me the Berkeley number, which I put on the calendar. He had an appointment at three and said he'd probably be late because of the traffic. He told me not to worry, and when he didn't make it home that night, I reported all this to the campus police. They referred me to the city police."

Nicole surprised us both by hugging her mom. "Thank you. I'm sorry he's missing, but I'm so grateful you told me what you know. Have you found out what happened to the UC bookstore?"

"A lot of books and tablets and computers were crushed. I think he was in the manager's office on the second floor, and I'm not sure…" Her voice shook. I looked at Nicole whose gaze was focused on her mother. "I'm not sure it withstood the quake. The firefighters said they cleared the building. They got a lot of people out, but not … not your dad as far as I know."

"So, nobody knows if he's alive?" I asked, even though I wasn't supposed to be a part of this conversation.

Mrs. Lorca looked at the ground, then up. "It's been almost a week."

"People have been trapped in mines longer. It's not too late to hope," I said quietly.

She shook her head and said, "I need to see what the boys are doing. It's too quiet up there."

I dropped onto a kitchen chair, sighing. This was so much worse than the possibility that we might not get to do the show.

"Mom, I know you're scared that Dad's dead," Nicole called after her, "but let me help." She was out of sight when I overheard her say, "I'm not the girl who drove drunk, and you need to realize that's in the past. Sandee trusts me and she's helping us. Ms. G and all my other teachers trust me."

"But Nicole…"

"One day at a time, remember? One day at a time, Dad is alive until he's not. If we're a family, we should be able to share our beliefs instead of shutting each other off in this icy silence."

Then I heard her mom say, "You're not as grown up as you think you are."

Nicole wasn't about to quit. "We need to be able to talk to each other. That's what a family does even if something terrible happens. Ask Sandee. She went through all kinds of bad stuff when her brother died, but she and her parents still talked."

Hearing her desperation, I tried to imagine what it would be like if my dad were buried in a bunch of rubble that used to be a bookstore. It was even worse than thinking about Bri. There was a lot of silence, and I couldn't decide whether to slip out the back door or stay in case Nicole needed to talk. When she came back in the kitchen, her eyes were filled with tears. "I am so sorry, Nicole. What can I do?"

"I know you want to help, but Mom and I need to be alone right now. I'll call you later," she said, staring out the kitchen window.

"If you don't call me, I'm going to call you." She looked

puzzled. "Friends do that, you know," I said as I turned the door knob.

What could I say that wouldn't make the situation worse? There was no reason to say how horrible it was that her dad was missing or how sad it was that her mom treated her like a needy little girl. She already knew. How could such a talented girl come from such a messed-up family?

A few minutes later as I pulled into our driveway, my phone buzzed, and I knew I had a text. I put on the brake and turned off the engine before I touched it. Mom said, **There's a new text from Dr. Henderson.**

**Okay, Mom. I'll be right in.** First though, I saw a text from Ms. G. **To everyone working on** *Our Town*: **Dr. Henderson says clean up must be complete before classes or activities can resume. The show is on hold.**

**Can students help?** I texted back.

**Probably not until the spills in the chem lab are cleaned up, the two buildings off their foundations have been removed, and all broken glass is gone. Will let you know if I hear anything different,** she wrote.

I sent her a sad face emoticon. Then I asked **You okay?**

**Yes, but I miss my drama students and especially the cast of** *Our Town*.

Bet Bowen would never say anything like that. I imagined her sitting at the piano. What did she think about as she played her songs?

**Thanks for the update. Do you need me to forward the message?**

**Sent to everyone, but thanks.**

I sent her a thumbs up emoji. I was sure she had other people to talk to.

"I'm afraid I already know, but what's in the principal's message?" I asked as soon as I walked into the kitchen.

"He said that there was a lot of damage in the science wing

and broken glass in the older classrooms. It's all got to be cleaned up, and someone from the county must sign off on the clean-up, and the new portables need to be placed on piers before students can return. The county has asked all school principals to wait until we go forty-eight hours without …"

Spike was running in circles in the backyard, and he barked so frantically that Mom and I could barely hear each other. Less than a minute later, the cabinet doors banged like an angry poltergeist invading our house. I ran outside ahead of Mom. The leaves twisted in the wind, and the lawn chairs shook as if the earth was battling itself below them. "This is more than an aftershock," I told Mom. "For all we know it's a whole new earthquake."

She nodded, with tears in her eyes, and I put my arms around her.

"Why don't they stop?"

"The quakes? You're asking the wrong person, honey. I have a horrible feeling that we're heading into uncertain times, what with global warming and all. I'm afraid this is beyond our control."

I'd already thought that a thousand times. For the second time today, there were no words to solve the problem. Instead, we hugged each other again, and I was grateful for her trust.

# PART TWO

Ten Days Later

# Chapter 14

## Thursday, October 17

### The Community of San Ramos, California

Only a few leaves still clung to the Sycamore branches. Usually that happens around Thanksgiving. We hadn't even celebrated Halloween yet. Even though two weeks had gone by, nothing seemed normal yet. In our part of town, aftershocks were now rare. Local reporters moved on, leaving us with no school, no social life, and some dangerously depressed people.

Dad told me people we'd visited were waiting for insurance checks. Meanwhile San Ramos had turned into a partial ghost town. Empty houses and stores. Empty gyms and basketball courts. Empty library and rec center. The police, neighborhood patrols, and insurance agents, like Dad, kept checking for vandalism.

Bottom line? The crisis might be gone, but the changes were everywhere. Sterling's Groceries, Dave's Gas Station, and other businesses were boarded up. Most of the roads had lane closures and detour signs, and Diego's empty house had been patched but not repaired. I think Dad was watching for squatters. Tornados sometimes crush part of a town and leave other parts completely alone. Apparently swarms of earthquakes are like that. There was no pattern, and I wondered if this was going to be a new kind of normal.

    Dad's temper often shorted out now. Mom climbed back into her shell and watched lots of Lifetime movies since Alicia moved her back to two days a week. At least her store was still open four hours a day.

    I missed Ms. G. I even missed Bowen—well, not really—but I missed the kids that mouthed off in her class. They kept us entertained. I never thought I'd miss the jerks and goof-offs, but there's a hole inside me that needs filling, and it's deeper and wider than the gaps in the sidewalk. I'm lonely. I miss Diego and rehearsals and feeling needed.

    Watching my hometown deteriorate is like riding a roller coaster through a house of horrors—not that anyone's setting them up for Halloween this year. Too many real horrors for that. Maybe some people will be partying. Not me. Not this year.

    Not Nicole either. Why would she celebrate Halloween or the Day of the Dead when her father is presumed dead? They never found his body. She's holding out hope, just like we did when we waited for a call from the Army saying Bri was being shipped to a hospital in Germany. That call never came.

    Nicole knows about Tessa's sister, and I wonder if she's secretly imagining her dad lying in a hospital bed somewhere. Having a missing family member is so cruel. Ugly. Unfair. I never thought about the consequences when the big quake rocked our world. Back then it was an adrenaline rush. Even the gas fire that destroyed the Rivera's restaurant seems small now. It's the consequences that are huge.

    This was our family's first Halloween since Bri died. I've heard that the Day of the Dead brings spirits to visit the living. If Diego were still next door, I'd ask him if it's true, but he's in Fallon, and asking, "Is the Day of the Dead real?" over the phone seems weird. If we were face-to-face, I could say, "Just kidding" if he rolled his eyes, but the way we are now he could could laugh at my text and share it with his new friends.

Guess I'll light a candle in case Bri wants to contact me. Apparently, that makes it easier for people on the other side to communicate with us. I want to make it easy if there's anything Bri has to say.

On his first day at Churchill County High School, Diego texted, There's one high school in this whole county. Grim. Then he added It's good I speak Spanish, cause nobody can talk about me or pretend they don't speak English when I'm around. Some kids do that whether the new people are teachers or Anglo kids. I was heartbroken when he celebrated his sixteenth birthday without me and sent me a picture of his Nevada license. I sent him an applause emoji, followed by a kiss emoji. If he got it, he didn't say anything.

His English teacher, who also directs the plays, picks shows with parts for everyone who auditions. Not sure I'd want to be in a show without earning a part.

At least Pete is still here. Too bad I can't find him anywhere. When we're together, he holds my hand or puts his arm around my shoulder, and the kids we walk past look at me like I'm a cheerleader. When he ignores me, though, it hurts. Where does he go when he disappears? Does he walk away because of something I've said or done? I'm going to ask him the next time he's sitting at Starbucks staring at his phone. Maybe I'll even ask him what he's looking at on that thing.

Tessa still collects clothes for displaced people. Red-tagged homes run up and down I-80, and there are some here too. It must be so hard to leave the place where you live with nothing but the clothes on your back and maybe your devices.

What if some of the kids who live on the Hayward fault change schools and we get a bunch of new students living with relatives?

My mind won't stop spinning. Reminds me of my anxiety after Bri's funeral. Headaches pounded behind my eyes back then, and they started up again after the quake. Mom asked if I needed to see a doctor, but I told her we had Tylenol. She rolled her eyes. I walked away. She doesn't see why I can't move past the ladder incident. How do I stop reliving that sensation that I'm about to drop through a hole, and nothing will ever be the same?

I almost told Mom, "Look how long it took you to get over Bri's death," but I'm not sure she is or ever will be. Besides I don't want to hurt her. She's been hurt enough. So have I. I just want things back the way they were before Bri joined the Army.

Right now, I'm staring at San Ramos High through a chain link fence. There are stacks of soil filled with roots and cement chunks in the quad, piles of computer parts, paint jars, and containers of animals in formaldehyde tossed around. The whole place looks desolate, and the workmen play their radios and joke around like our loss means nothing to them.

I just took some photos from a distance, plus a close up of Dr. Henderson in a t-shirt and jeans, patrolling between the science building and the gym. My long shots of the tipsy buildings didn't do their weird angles justice, so I walked up Main Street in the leafy sunlight searching for a shot that would show how much we've lost. Maybe the photos will matter someday. Maybe I'm recording history, but what will future generations do with the knowledge that an earthquake disrupted life in the first quarter of the twenty-first century?

I stared at the cracks zigzagging down the sidewalk, but the only way I could show the devastation in one photo would be to take a long shot of Alvarado Street where the gas pipe burst and burned up the Rivera's restaurant and the stores around it. There's lots of scarred timber, stacked in messy heaps, and everything's protected by caution tape, but nothing captures the drama and tension. It's alive in my nerve endings, but I can't photograph them.

When I got to San Ramos Park, I heard the screeches of grade school kids shouting as they chased each other in a crazy game of tag. Other kids sat on a cement ledge staring at nothing. Only a handful of parents stood around, probably sharing neighborhood horror stories. More caution tape kept everybody off the swings and the jungle gym. I took a picture of that, too, because I'd never seen caution tape on a playground before.

A bunch of kids who were probably freshmen sat around a wooden picnic table. They wore earbuds and passed their phones around showing what they'd found on Instagram or Snapchat or TikTok. A tall boy at the end of the table waved at me.

Hard to believe what I saw. "Pete! Too busy to return my texts?" Admittedly I was teasing, but I was also testing him. What excuse would he invent today?

The kids at the table stared at the two of us. An argument between upperclassmen would make their day, but I wasn't going to give them anything to film and post. Pete said, "You know. A guy gets busy."

Moving closer, I got a whiff of him. "Whew! When was the last time you showered?" I heard a laugh that sounded like Tony's but I didn't see him.

Pete glared at the laughing boy and said, "The water's off in our apartment."

"Why didn't you call me? You could have used ours." The kids leaned in, eager to catch every word.

"Uh, okay. Do you mean now?" Pete grabbed his backpack, and said, "Catch you later, guys," before I could answer him. "Got that car you were driving in on Saturday?" he asked as we walked away.

"That was my mom's car. Dad's is still at the Oakland Airport. The road out there is closed, so we're all using Mom's car."

"Good parents," he said. His face was like a mask—emotionless.

I hoped he was right. Both my parents were at work, so I was taking a boy to use our shower, and no one would be home but me, but either one of them could come in at any time. If they smelled him, they'd know it was a worthy cause. Maybe it was fine to have boys over now that I was sixteen. Maybe I worried way too much. Being with Pete gave me courage. Or maybe my instincts had changed.

We were headed for Sycamore Avenue before I said, "How do you know so many of the younger kids?"

He shrugged as he said, "You know."

I didn't, but I had no intention of admitting it, so instead I said, "You haven't told me anything about your parents, Pete."

"Dad sells used cars. So does Mom. Lots of competition between them."

"Do you have brothers or sisters?"

"Big sister."

"Maybe your whole family would like to use our shower."

"Sis is away at college. USC. Mom and Dad aren't home right now."

His choppy answers reminded me of Diego. He spoke like that when he'd had a difficult day. Of course, Diego's snappy answers made me imagine he had rhythms running through his head. Pete was different. His answers were short and abrupt for no reason I could think of. He acted like I was his girl until I asked about his family. Then he shut me out and threw away the key. As I opened our front door, I wondered what he was hiding, but I couldn't figure out how to ask him when he obviously didn't want to answer.

"Anybody home?" When we didn't hear an answer I said, "The shower's upstairs. I'll get you a clean towel."

"You're sweet," he said, and the likeable Pete I met at Starbucks on the day before the big earthquake was back. I stayed upstairs while he showered. My heart was fluttering, being alone in the house with a boy who was taking a shower right next to my bedroom.

While I waited for him, I saw Tia Wong's e-mail, asking me questions for a story about how teens were coping with the earthquake's disruptions. How exciting was that? Something made her ask me instead of any other high school junior. That mattered, though I could not explain why.

I couldn't wait to tell Diego and Nicole—and maybe Pete—but first I wrote back, "I'm good but avoiding ladders for a while. School's closed and a horrible thing happened to my friend, Nicole. She's one of the stars in the play, remember? Her father didn't come home after the quake. Nobody knows what happened to him. I know he's not the only parent who's missing, but could you tell that story?"

Had I overdone it? I added, "We're a lot better off than Hayward or San Leandro or any towns directly over the fault, but everybody has stories right now."

Someone was watching me, and I started to say, "Bri, are you..." but instead I looked up and realized Pete stood in the doorway rubbing a towel across his wet hair. He wasn't wearing a shirt, and his deltoids and pecs rippled. He could model for the cover of any romance novel.

"You look so hot, sitting there," he said. I glanced down and saw my cleavage pushing up into the V-neck of my purple tee. I must have blushed because he said, "Don't be embarrassed. Now that Diego's moved ..."

"Diego wasn't my boyfriend."

"And there's nobody else?"

I shook my head without looking up and skimmed my e-mail. My cheeks burned. I was afraid to look at him.

"Before long, you'll have one." When I didn't say anything, he added, "What are you writing?"

"Answering an e-mail. I talked to an intern/reporter on the day the quake nearly knocked me off the ladder. She said that people want to know more."

I could smell the scent of Mom's lavender soap when he leaned over to read what I was writing. "Hope she did a video interview with you, sweetie."

How I wanted to pull his face toward mine and kiss his mouth. Not yet, I told myself, wondering where that thought popped up from. Calmly, I said, "We did a video chat."

Did he want to kiss me as badly as I wanted to kiss him?

"I'll bet plenty of people saw you. That's probably why people are writing in. Bet some foxy dudes are looking for a hook-up. Why don't you ask this intern person if she'd like to come out and do a story on the school? Or the play? Or your family?" Pete asked.

Okay. So, he was an organizer like me. He didn't have any idea he was driving me crazy. Unless he was playing hard to get. He shouldn't be telling me what to say. The last thing I needed was to become dependent on a guy who drove me crazy, gave me great ideas, and then ignored me for days.

He leaned in until his cheek, rough with spots of stubble, grazed mine. A shiver ran through me.

We both heard the whir of the garage door and he jumped back. "Leave," I said as my heart thumped into my ribs.

"Why?"

"My parents are home."

"So what? We aren't doing anything, are we?" I tossed him

his shirt and pointed.

"You sending me out the front door?"

"They're coming in from the garage. Grab your stuff and get out of here before Dad kicks you out."

He stood there, grinning, until I screamed, "Just go!"

His feet pounded down the stairs. My throat ached. A minute later the front door slammed. The house was silent for a good two minutes. Then I heard a familiar creak as the front door opened. What was it about "leave" that Pete couldn't understand?

"We're back, Sandee," Mom called, "and look who we found right outside."

"Hi, Sandee. How ya doin'?" Pete asked.

My eyes widened as I looked at his innocent face and his misbuttoned shirt. He'd convinced them he was arriving and probably explained his wet hair by saying he'd come over after showering in his parents' apartment. What a silver-tongue manipulator.

"Pete's going to stay for dinner so the two of you can work ahead and really surprise Ms. Bowen." Dad's statement didn't surprise me a bit.

"Sure. Why not? We'll get back to school someday." If my parents were home, I could take advantage of his math skills without worrying that he might grab me and hold me with a deep kiss while his hands roamed. Or I could close the door to the family room and let it happen if ... No! When did I get so indecisive?

"Before you go to work, do you want some pizza?" Mom asked.

"Sure." We said it together.

"Sandee, can you set the table?"

While I got the silverware, Pete said, "Sounds delicious. So how are those insurance claims going Mr. Mason?" I couldn't figure out Pete's game, but it was kind of fun to watch a high

107

school boy wrap my parents around his little finger.

We were finishing dinner when my phone beeped. Jenn texted, It's been forty-eight hours since we've even had a tremor, so what's the new rehearsal schedule?

I wrote back, Haven't heard. Want to invite the leads over so we can run lines?

Great idea, Sandee. Group text! Let's meet at my place in half an hour. Jenn was totally focused on the show again while Pete was totally go-with-the-flow. I felt trapped and squeezed by her next message. You'll be there, right?

I read it out loud, and before Mom or Dad could say a word, Pete said, "Jenn sure is pushy."

"Persistent," I said. Nobody disagreed. "Maybe we could work on math tomorrow? This is important."

Mom and Dad looked at each other. "I guess so, as long as you do it. Pete, is your car here?"

"Nope."

"Sandee, why don't you drop him off on your way to Jenn's?"

I stood up and said, "Let's go, Pete. You can finally show me where you live."

"See ya," he called over his shoulder on our way out.

## Chapter 15

"Where are we going?" I asked Pete as I pulled out of the garage.

"To Jenn's house. I'm going to find out what a San Ramos High rehearsal is like."

My fingers drummed on the steering wheel, and I gave him a Bowen-like stare. "Right or left. Where's your apartment?"

"You don't want to be late for rehearsal, Foxy Lady." Odd that he'd say that when he wouldn't even look at me.

"Please tell me where you live so we can get going."

"Let me go to rehearsal with you."

"Are you kidding? We aren't ready for an audience. The cast would be so uncomfortable with you there, so I have to drop you somewhere. Should I turn right or left?"

"Drop me at uhh… why don't you take me over to Jacob's, okay?"

"Jacob?"

"Diego used to go there for band practice, remember?"

"Do you know the address?"

"Don't you?"

"He lives a couple blocks over, but I don't remember which house," I said.

"Take me a couple blocks over and I'll walk. I've got a really good memory and I'll recognize the house."

Pressing my lips together, I pulled up on the corner of Old Creek and Ash. Let him walk if that's what he wanted.

"Thanks," he said as opened the door. The wind pressed into

his jacket, and he shuddered. Why did he refuse to let me drop him outside his apartment? I didn't expect him to ask me in. He acted like there was some hidden neighborhood in San Ramos I'd never seen, which was totally ridiculous.

"You're welcome," I said too quietly for him to hear.

He waved and called out, "See ya soon," as he slammed the door shut. I headed for the street, then changed my mind and circled around the block, but he wasn't there when I drove down Ash again, so he must have found the right house—or garage.

At Jenn's house, everyone was chatting about who they'd seen, who they hadn't seen, and especially what they'd heard since school closed. Jenn clapped her hands to get our attention and said, "Sandee, you read in the parts for anybody who isn't here, and let's see if we can get through Act II, okay everybody?" She sounded like our new director. Her stage husband nodded. So did her stage son, Tony, his eyes eager.

My hands trembled as I pulled out my script. Jenn was the real foxy lady. Not me. Why had I believed Pete earlier? His compliments felt like jabs now that he wasn't with me. Jenn was a size 2 to my size 12. She wore a tight-fitting tee and butt-hugging jeans, and as usual her makeup was perfect. I dressed to hide my body and when something clung to my ribs or thighs, stubborn bulges rippled under the cloth. I was hard working and creative sometimes, but nobody called me sexy. Pete was such a liar.

Jenn's sexy look and walk gave her built-in power. No wonder she was so confident. I'd seen girls who acted like her on TV, and a minute ago I'd watched her tell the whole cast what to do. Diego would have understood and might have reminded me that we were in her house, so I should cut her some slack, but right now she made me want to pounce. Instead, I said, "Ready to start us off, Nicole?" while struggling to keep my voice non-judgmental so Jenn wouldn't have a new reason to pick on me.

"Three years have gone by," Nicole began, and as she took us into the story, I let my mind wander. Where would I be in three years? Majoring in drama on a UC campus or studying some subject I hadn't discovered yet? Would I be an Army private like Bri or was that crazy? Would I leave the state and move far away from earthquake country or stay in California somewhere far away from the faults?

What happened in the dorms at UC Berkeley when an earthquake hit? Books tumbled? Pictures swayed? Rugs slid? Windows rattled? Branches pierced right through them?

"Line?" Nicole asked.

"It's July 7th."

Nicole shook her head, and Jenn said, "She just did that, Sandee. Are you following the script or not?"

I ignored her and skipped to the next paragraph. "That's the time most of our..."

"Got it," Nicole said. "That's the time most of our young people jump up and get married."

Getting married was an option I hadn't considered. When Diego left, I knew he'd miss me, but that didn't make me the girl of his dreams. Pete talked sexy, but he'd turned into a puzzle on steroids. Besides he was too independent. Like Bowen, who never got married. Neither did Ms. G, as far as I knew. Did she wish she was married or was she quiet about her divorce—maybe from an actor who couldn't earn a living?

I glanced at the script. I'd have to fill in for Howie Newsome and Si Crowell, but when they talked to each other, I'd tell Jenn to go to her next line. She'd like that. Maybe she'd stop one-upping me.

The cast was pushing through, going faster than they would on stage. As I said Mrs. Soames' last line, "The important thing is to be happy," we heard a familiar rumbling pumping through the foundation below the McCall's Persian carpet. The ceiling fan over their marble and wood table swayed wider and wider until I was afraid it would fall. An old-fashioned Crosley radio toppled off a bookcase, pushing Bradley to the floor. Jenn scrambled under a big table in front of the couches, along with every other actor who could fit, while Nicole raced to the nearest doorframe. I covered my head with my hands and the script.

Gusts of wind came hurtling toward the front windows, which shook and rattled. A big branch snapped and flew through the front window. It sailed past the table Jenn was under, sending shards of glass into the carpet. Then splat! Glass landed next to me with a loud thunk. Maria shrieked at the same moment Tony did, though they were on opposite sides of the room.

"Here we go again." Jenn said. I looked up and saw tears smearing her make up. We hid from the wrath of nature for what seemed like thirty minutes but was probably thirty seconds.

"What do we do now?" Nicole asked.

I shook my head. Everybody's concentration was destroyed along with the chance that we'd be back in school by Monday. Quietly I said, "Thanks for trying, Jenn, but everybody's too upset to keep going."

"What's wrong with you guys?" she asked, turning from side to side like a politician seeking votes.

"Another aftershock could happen any minute," Nicole said. Her fear was deep—probably because her father was missing.

"And I can't think about anything but biking home on a street that might open up and swallow me," said Tony.

"Or the fact that school won't open on Monday," Bradley

added, squirming his way out from under the bulky radio. "Jenn, we're here in your living room because we can't use the theater and we've only got three weeks until this thing's supposed to open."

"I should have called Ms. G," Jenn said as if she couldn't process another quake.

"Having her here wouldn't have stopped the aftershocks," Nicole said.

Jenn opened her mouth, but I said, "Nicole's right. None of us control the earthquakes or the wind."

Jenn burst into tears again. "Okay, guys. Go home. This isn't meant to be," she said between sobs. Bradley and Nicole both went to console her.

Others gathered up jackets and backpacks and scripts. I hated that Jenn was right, but objectives barely existed, reactions weren't realistic, and we hadn't started working on pace, flow, or three-dimensionality. Even though I didn't want to say anything, I knew we weren't going to be ready for opening night—not that it mattered if we didn't have a theatre.

## Chapter 16

### Monday, October 21

### The Mason's House

Before dawn my eyes popped open, and I sat straight up in bed. Tree branches danced in the moonlight and a streetlight elongated the shadows falling across my closet door. Did another earthquake wake me up or was I having nightmares again?

When Bri went missing, I often dreamed about an explosion followed by a fire. The same fire, blazing in desert sand, occurred night after night. Not so different from aftershocks, which rolled through, increasing the destruction, and leaving us unable to put our lives back together. Nobody's life was destroyed, at least no one I knew, though Diego's and Nicole's families had been badly hurt.

There was no way I could stop the flames in my dreams or the earthquakes ripping up and down the San Francisco Bay Area. This dream slid away so quickly that I wondered if it was something new or an old rerun. The whole block where the Rivera's restaurant once stood was nothing more than a pile of ashes, rubble, and caution tape. Pete's family had no water and aftershocks kept taking the power out. Being so powerless was the ultimate frustration.

The covers shifted without my moving. Looking over, I smiled at the big brown eyes staring up at me. I reached out and nuzzled Spike's furry ears. "Can you remember another time like this, Spike? I'm trying to figure out a way I can get us out of this mess. Any ideas?" He gave a soft growl but didn't take his eyes off me. "We need to get some sleep big guy."

If he could have spoken English he would have asked, "Where's Bri?" They say dogs never forget.

The next thing I knew sunshine streamed through the slats of my mini blinds.

When I walked into the kitchen half an hour later, Dad sat alone drinking coffee, eating a bear claw, and watching our local news. Plant-based nutrition is not his thing. Mine either. A bear claw sounded delicious. I pulled one out of the bakery bag, breaking it in two so I wouldn't pack on the pounds.

After two bites, I looked at the news which was on the mini-TV in the kitchen and saw Tia Wong standing next to a building with the right-side dipping into the earth. Holding the mic up to her mouth, she said, "The scientists at UC Berkeley's Seismology Lab are as puzzled as the rest of us. No one understands why aftershocks keep rolling along California's fault lines or why the wind picks up when the fault lines rumble. A few scientists theorize that the earth is fighting back against global warming. Others say this is the reverse of the ice age. What we see before us is evidence of the impact that climate change is having on California's citizens."

"Do you think she's right, Dad?" I asked once the TV channel went to a commercial.

"I don't understand any more than that reporter does, but it's important to stay informed and watch the trends. Are you ready to make the rounds with me and meet some of my clients?"

Guess he hadn't given up on teaching me a lesson. "I'm going over to the school and see if I can help get the theatre ready in time for the show." Before he could remind me that kids weren't allowed on campus, I added, "I know they said we couldn't help, but it's not like I want to mess with spilled chemicals in the science and art wings."

"Your willingness to help is admirable," he said as he picked up his dishes and set them in the sink.

"Thanks, Dad."

"Switching subjects, Pete seems quite interested in you."

"Uh...yeah." I sounded like Pete with my short answer, but if Dad knew about Pete's disappearing acts, he'd tell me to stay away. I wasn't ready for that. Mom saved me. She came stumbling into the kitchen in her robe and slippers and headed straight for the coffee pot. After a long, slow sip, she pulled her phone out of her robe pocket and said, "We got more information from Dr. Henderson, Sandee."

She handed me her phone, which said, Last night's aftershock, which registered 6.5 on the Richter scale, may have been totally separate from the original earthquake.

A scarier part came next:

Though every school program matters, academics come first. Because we need to rebuild the science wing and replace damaged textbooks, and because of the serious funding issues this district has faced over the last three years, we can no longer provide financial support for co-curricular activities including all sports, clubs, yearbook, newspaper, music, and drama. We regret having to shut these programs down mid-season, but other schools in surrounding districts are in the same position.

Once we have funded the science wing and the textbook purchases, we'll reassess. Meanwhile, there are community outlets where your boys and girls can pursue activities. I hope we'll all be together and back in school soon.

The back of my neck tightened into spasms, and a headache throbbed behind my eyes. "He can't do that."

"I don't think it's up to you. You'll have to find other outlets, like he suggested?" Mom said.

"But *Our Town* is already in rehearsal. The yearbook's laid out, I think. And what about Mr. Jackson's Winter Concert? Henderson can't just pull the plug on everything."

"Calm down, Sandee," Dad said. "He wouldn't do this if he had a choice." Before I could answer, he took a final slurp of coffee, grabbed his briefcase, and said, "Time to make some calls and assess the latest damage. This earthquake has made a mess of far more than your school play."

"I've gotta text Nicole. And Jenn. And maybe the whole cast, though Ms. G's probably already doing that." It surprised me that there wasn't a message from her yet.

Mom sipped from a coffee cup Bri made in Scouts, and a faraway look settled on her face. I set her phone on the placemat and began texting on mine: **Henderson's canceled all EC activities. What are we going to do?** I typed in Nicole's name, then Jenn's, and then I thought, why not send this to the whole cast? I clicked on Ms. G's last group message to all of us, changed the subject, pasted my question in, and hit send.

Jenn texted right back. **He can't do that. The coaches won't let him. Brb.** I finished my bear claw, then wandered to the refrigerator. For once I was too upset to be hungry, but I wanted comfort food to nibble on.

Nicole checked in next. **Mom says the boys' soccer team at their elementary school is cancelled. She's calling the district office.**

So far there was nothing from Tony, Amber, Bradley, or any other cast members except Maria, who sent the question that was on everybody's mind: **What do we do now?**

Her freshman year was disappearing before her eyes and her extended family now lived in Fallon, Nevada. **We'll figure something out**, I texted, though I didn't have a clue how we'd do that.

No sooner had I hit send than I realized I had more to say, so I wrote, **What would Diego say if he were still here?** I hit delete and rewrote: **…if he still lived here**. We were in enough trouble without phrasing it like he'd died.

As soon as I hit send again, I called Diego, who picked up immediately and asked, "What's up?"

"You'll never guess what Henderson's done," I said without even asking him how he was. Before he could say a word, I grabbed Mom's phone, which was sitting on the table while she kept staring at the same cup while reading Henderson's message.

"Bummer. So, what's the plan? Cause I know you have one."

"Not yet. That's why I'm calling. You have amazing ideas sometimes, so can you tell me how we can raise money and find a venue? And how can you talk on your phone during school? Do you have a sub?"

"It's a teacher in-service day. I'm in my room—sorry, our room--hiding from everybody and their bickering."

"What?" A chill ran up my spine.

"I'm a guest in my little cousin's room. The lower bunk is all mine along with half the closet, one dresser drawer and one desk drawer. My drums are in the basement."

"That sounds awful. I'm so sorry. What does his room look like? I should have FaceTimed you so I could see for myself."

"He's got posters for *Diary of a Wimpy Kid* and

*Goosebumps.* It's like a middle school torture chamber."

"He's a reader?"

"I haven't seen him with a book yet. Probably his mom bought them."

"So, what else is in the room?"

"We have a window looking out on sand and sagebrush. No trees. There's only one teeny park in the whole town, and the only band in the high school marches at the football games." After a big sigh he added, "This isn't how our junior year was supposed to go."

"You've got that right." I imagined him scrunched on the lower bunk with his shoulders forward and the wire spirals on the bunk above him nearly touching his head. "Do you have any place where you can be alone?"

"Well, the bathroom door locks."

"TMI!"

"Seriously, Sandee. Is the Little Theatre trashed?"

My neck muscles tightened. "They're not letting anyone in. There could be loose boards and shards from mirrors. The lights could have fallen, or a wall might have caved in—just like your kitchen."

"I get it. You can't perform on campus but there might be someplace else."

"That's why I called. What have you got in mind?"

"The community center or a church? Why don't you ask this incredibly cool chick we both know? Sandee Mason. She's the stage manager, and rumor has it that she can fix anything," he said in the mock parent voice he adopted after *Oklahoma!* closed. He stopped his role-play as he said, "So, what are you doing right now to keep the show from falling apart?"

"We ran lines for Act II at Jenn's house last night until

another aftershock brought a tree crashing through her front window. Did I tell you Henderson said it might be a whole new earthquake and not an aftershock at all?"

"You mentioned it. So, until you can get back on campus, there's no rush to get the show ready, right? Just keep going over lines and ask Jenn's parents if you can rent the Children's Theatre when you're ready to perform. They'll probably donate the space for a good cause. Or have Ms. G ask."

"Seriously? We need a real stage, not a kid's stage where our heads would practically bump the stage lights." Diego was a musician at heart, and his San Ramos band could perform anywhere. They didn't have to worry about blocking or relationships, and they could even have their music and lyrics in front of them.

As I was thinking that he said, "There aren't any sets, right?"

"Right."

"So do some mic checks and go with the lighting they have. You could do it in a teen club if you had to."

"We don't have a teen club in San Ramos, remember? And it's a little more complicated than that."

"Well, if you're going to shoot down everything I say, why did you call?"

I could picture him running his hand through his hair the way he did when we worked on algebra. "Sorry. This has me really stressed. Do you suppose they have earthquakes in Grover's Corners, New Hampshire?"

"Why don't you ask Siri?"

"Good idea. You're full of them, you know. New subject: How's your mom doing now?"

"Better. She and my aunt are cooking a lot, which she loves, but whenever the news talks about all those aftershocks, she insists she's never going back."

"They're covering Bay Area news in Nevada?"

"Sure. It's a big story. The newscasters say it'll be years before the East Bay is back to normal. Dad wants to rent a new place in San Ramos and start over, but Mom says no." I refilled my apple juice glass while he hesitated. What was he having so much trouble saying? "Has anyone asked where I went?" he finally asked.

Guilt struck. I'd been so obsessed with the show's problems that I hadn't talked to anyone in his band. "A lot of them must be wondering about you," I said, hoping it was true. "Have you texted any of them?"

"I was waiting for them to text me, but that's not a bad idea." How I wished he could see my smile. "I miss you a lot, Sandee."

"Can you turn on FaceTime?"

"I don't want you to see this place. It makes it too hard to say good-bye."

"I miss you too." Saying those words, I realized how much I meant it. "So, have you found any new friends there?"

"It's hard when you transfer during the year. There is this one foxy chick…"

"Oh?"

"I didn't say we'd met, but she's as good-looking as you." Was this really Diego, who could barely put two words together? I was stunned into silence until he asked, "Did you hear me?"

Of course I heard him. Couldn't he hear my heart fluttering? "Yeah. Did you mean what you just said?"

"Yup. It's my awkward way of saying I can't meet new people unless you're around. I miss you. You can call anytime, but they take away our cells at school just like they do at home."

"If I could text you anytime, you'd never pay attention in

class."

"I'm too poor to pay attention."

"What?"

"There's this transfer student from Texas who says that every time the biology teacher tells him to pay attention. It was funny the first ten times I heard it."

"Did you know you have a beautiful voice, Diego?"

He sighed deeply. "I can't wait to get back home. Gotta go. My turdy little cousin is banging on the door."

"Bye. Love you," I added after he clicked off. I'd have said it, but I was afraid of driving him away. He was so much more sincere than Pete, and so much shyer. I keep hearing that boys mature more slowly than girls. If he was outgrowing his shyness, though, I wanted him to do it where I could watch. I missed him more than I realized.

Leaning back, I stared at the ceiling and considered renting the Children's Theatre. If we used it, would the music department expect to give their winter concert there? Would the student council or the debate club ask for it next time?

If Jenn came up with the idea herself, the cast might encourage her. If I suggested it, though, there'd be one hurdle after another. We'd had enough of those. There had to be a better solution.

My thoughts kept slipping back to Diego. How could he and Pete be so different? Was it just a matter of confidence or were there more basic issues?

# Chapter 17

## Tuesday, October 22

### Sandee's Home and Downtown San Ramos

"Mom, I'm going out," I said as I put my breakfast dishes in the sink. "Do you need anything?"

"You can walk Spike, but my car stays here, understood?"

Mom was in a mood, and I just wanted to be outside. Spike lay on the kitchen floor with his nose between his paws. I attached his leash, and he was the only one who saw me roll my eyes.

"Let's go by the library," I said as soon as we were outside. I loved feeling the sun on my skin and the wind running through my hair. You wouldn't mind waiting outside while I re-shelve some books, would you? They need help and I need to do something that doesn't involve listening to Mom complain."

He woofed, which meant, "Go for it, Sandee." All kinds of people volunteered these days—digging through rubble, donating supplies, and rebuilding broken walls. Since students couldn't help on campus, I'd share my skills elsewhere. I wanted to do more than take messages for Dad or get ahead in Bowen's class. For all I knew, she might be dead before we got back to school. Harsh but possible. She was pretty old.

Walking under the sycamores that morning with the sun shining through translucent yellow leaves, I couldn't help comparing Diego's mom to mine. Since Bri died, my mom had been an emotional wreck most of the time, like Mrs. Rivera when her house got damaged. Before the quake Mrs. Rivera worked six days a week in the restaurant. Before we got the news about Bri, my mom worked at Alicia's Antiques and donated her time to adult literacy. We knew why she got so depressed, but not why her depression kept popping up a day or two after we thought she was better. My psych teacher told us depression is anger turned inwards. That made sense in Mom's case. Today she was angry—maybe at Bri for dying or maybe at the earth for disrupting her post-Bri world. Maybe it's healthy that her anger's coming out instead of turning in, but I don't want to be in the line of fire.

Spike and I dodged acorns and amber balls as we made our way past the pocket park next to the library. I tied him to a green metal bench and left enough slack so he could sniff the bushes. Then I walked through the open door and scrawled my name across the sign-in sheet that sat on a clipboard at the registration desk. I heard soprano and alto chatter and immediately thought of 'Pick a little / Talk a little…' from *The Music Man*. This was no musical, though. This was real life.

I figured I could start anywhere, so I headed for the fiction section, but a woman with a lanyard around her neck and a pencil behind her ear stopped me and said, "May I help you?"

"I'm here to put books back on shelves, just like everybody else."

"That's very nice of you. May I see some ID?"

I loved fishing my driver's license out of my backpack. When the Lanyard Lady looked at it, she frowned. "Sorry, hon, but you're too young."

"Why? Who turns down free labor?"

"We don't have earthquake insurance so everyone helping

today signed a waiver," she explained.

"Okay. I'll sign. I already put my name on the clipboard."

"I'm sorry, miss, but you must be eighteen before you can sign a state waiver. We'd love to have your help, but it violates state law. It's not your fault you didn't know."

I folded my arms to match hers. "I thought everybody was pulling together to help out."

"They are, my dear. You just can't volunteer in a county or state-owned building. It's the law."

"Whatever." I turned on my heel and left her standing there.

Outside, I undid Spike's leash. "Let's walk down by the creek, Spike. Maybe I can find a frog that needs saving."

Sycamore Creek only had a drizzle running through the bottom in October. Brown grasses grew tall and thorny on its banks. As we walked, I replayed my last conversation with Nicole. Driving her home after the aborted rehearsal at Jenn's house, I asked how her family was doing. She stared at her hands and said, "Not great." Obviously, she was avoiding something, but as we turned the corner of her street, she said, "Can you pull over for a minute?"

"Jenn told me that Amber, who was cast as Emily Webb, said the Berkeley Police Department sent out notices to everyone who filed a missing person's report. It said, 'Those who have not heard from their loved ones need to consider the possibility that they might not have survived.'"

We both stared out the window at the lights coming from the houses on her street. "Your mom hasn't heard anything?"

"She won't say. I don't get it, Sandee. What is she hiding?"

"I don't have a clue. It's just a rumor, right?"

Nicole stared at her hands instead of looking at me. "I'm so worried that I can't think straight."

What would Mom and I do if we got the same message about Dad? I couldn't even guess, but she wouldn't pretend she hadn't heard anything.

"Mom insists Dad's a survivor," Nicole said. "She figures he dropped his phone as he ran out of the building. Since the buses weren't running, he couldn't get back home and without his phone he didn't have a way to call."

"So why didn't he borrow a phone? Isn't that what a grown up would do?" We both knew Mrs. Lorca was grasping at straws. I remembered hoping Bri was okay until the Army notified us, but Mrs. Lorca acted like the police refused to search, which had to be denial. If her dad didn't come home, how would Nicole and her mom cope?

I only had to look at Mom and Dad to know how much they'd suffered, but I didn't know how to help Nicole. "I'm so sorry," I finally said in a small voice. She teared up then, which wasn't like her at all, so I added, "You'll get through this. Waiting is tough."

I handed her a Kleenex and let her sob. When she quieted, I touched her hand and she said, "Don't worry. I'm a survivor—just like Dad."

I nodded because I couldn't speak. My throat closed up thinking about how much loss we'd both gone through in the last seven months.

Spike tugged on the leash, and I remembered we were supposed to be walking. I'd stopped moving and he had no idea why. "Sorry, Spike. Let's make sure some kid isn't playing with matches around all that dry brush because he had nothing better to do while his parents are at work." The last thing we needed was another fire after what happened to the Rivera's restaurant, followed by Kubler's, and Sportsmen Unite. There'd been enough tragedy in San Ramos this year.

    Crickets chirped and bullfrogs croaked as Spike and I waded through the prickly weeds growing on the creek bank. We were almost to the freeway overpass when something grabbed my left foot, bit through my sock, and held on tight. I fought it, struggling to get free. Then I fell. Hard. Riding the ladder flashed through my head as thick, scratchy grasses raked across my bare ankles and arms. I sneezed and gasped. Thistles scratched my cheek.

    "Spike!" I screamed. He woofed. Clumps of weeds, roots, and soil wrapped around my ankle and kept me pinned to the ground. I slid further, the clump yanking at my ankle. Beneath me I thought I felt the earth roll. Was this an aftershock? A foreshock? Another new quake? I couldn't tell any more.

    With my eyes closed I screamed, "Help" at the top of my lungs. The ground dipped. I'd rolled into a hole. Or a ditch. My nose was now up against a bumpy barrier. I sniffed, like Spike would have, and the musty odor brought back seventh grade memories. Diego and I used to meet up after school at some old, musty log near the creek that ran close to our houses.

    A rough tongue licked my cheek and lips. "What the… Spike. Let me get up."

    I shifted my torso, got up on one elbow, saw my foot trapped in a snarl of tree roots, moss, weeds, and leaves. Hard as I tried, I couldn't wriggle it out. Spike rushed to the rescue.

    Chew.

    Howl.

    Repeat.

    He was determined to free me, and I worried that he'd wind up with a mouthful of stickers. He dug his teeth into the snarl of roots until we both heard a snap. "No," I screamed. Which bone snapped?

Undeterred, Spike offered me a mouthful of broken roots as I reached for my swollen foot.

"What's going on down there," a deep voice called. Footsteps clomped through the grass, and I imagined a police officer in thick black boots stomping down the hill to rescue me. The boots were actually Reebok's. Officers don't wear jeans with holes in the knees. I looked up as Pete announced, "I'm your rescue committee." I didn't need to be protected or saved, but I loved the way his hand brushed my ankle as he tackled the rest of the weeds.

Spike yapped, and Pete reached out to pet him. "It's okay, Spike," I told him, but he wouldn't stop growling until Pete took his hand back. He's usually a good judge of character and I didn't understand his growls until I remembered the night Pete refused to let me drop him off at his apartment. Then again, maybe Pete stank again. Pete wrapped his warm hands around my foot then ran them up and down both the foot and leg. Carefully he poked at my ankle looking for swelling.

"Did you get first aid training when you were a lifeguard?"

He looked into my eyes as he pulled the sticky weeds off my shoulders and said, "How could you tell? I never told you I was a lifeguard."

I pulled away and said, "You know what you're doing." There was something edgy and dangerous about him that appealed, but it scared me when his hands kept moving up my leg, stroking it softly.

I put my shoe back on and he helped me stand up. Then he reached out to pet Spike, who showed his teeth. "Maybe Spike keeps growling because I smell grungy to him," Pete said.

"Still no water at your place?"

"Nope. There are more urgent needs than our plumbing

problems." He put his arms around my shoulder protectively, and asked, "Why are you and Mr. Grumpy here?"

My sigh was loud, like the winds that had been blowing through the valley. "His name is Spike, and we're out because …" I didn't know what to say. "We're out to get away from … you know—everything." I didn't add that no one would let me pick up books and put them back on the library shelves. "I could ask you the same thing."

He looked straight ahead as he said, "Waiting for school to restart." His chin was speckled with the start of a beard.

"Your parents let you just roam around town?"

"I'm a guy. It's different for a girl."

"Are you trying to get a rise out of me?"

He laughed and said, "That's no way to thank a guy." Then he put his hand on my back, pulled me to him, and kissed me. Not a peck, but a real kiss.

Something came over me when he did that, and I kissed him back, despite his disgusting smell.

"Better," he said, "Can I help you to your car, gentle lady? I know you can get there on your own, but please let me make sure you're safe."

I brushed the remaining weeds off my clothes, shook the dust out of my hair, and said, "Thank you, kind sir."

No response. He acted like nothing had happened. A moment later I said, "Really, Pete, why are you down here?"

"Sandee, you ask too many questions. Can I take you for a cup of coffee?"

"I don't get it. How come you have nothing to do other than go for coffee?"

He shrugged and said, "That was quite a tumble you took. You don't suppose there was another aftershock, do you?"

"Didn't your parents show you Henderson's latest e-mail?"

"Didn't see it," he mumbled as we shuffled through piles of sycamore leaves that covered the sidewalk. "What did he say?"

"Everything's on hold until we have forty-eight-hours without an aftershock. I can't believe your parents didn't tell you."

"They're kind of busy." He took my dirt-stained arm and said, "Your car's in the lot on the other side of the library, right?"

"Spike and I walked here. Mom's going to worry if we don't get back. Could you drive us?"

Pete shook his head again. He sure got quiet sometimes.

"Okay. We can walk it. My ankle doesn't really hurt."

"Can I walk with the two of you?"

"I have to get home. My parents don't trust me right now, remember?"

"No problem." It was though. He sounded distant—either hurt or distracted. It was hard to tell.

"If I fall into the weeds again, I hope you'll be around. Nobody else came near." I knew I was putting out signals, and I wasn't sure why. Maybe it was the chemistry they talk about in romance novels.

"Maybe it means we're meant to be together." He winked at me.

"Pete, I don't understand you. I'm trying to find ways to be useful, and you're … like … totally indifferent. What's up with that?"

He shrugged, which was not a satisfactory answer. He was an amazingly cool guy except when he shut down like he had an on-off switch. Something didn't add up, and I couldn't pinpoint it.

I stared for a minute, but he had nothing more to say, and

Spike was tugging at the leash. "Well, thanks for showing up when I needed you. Spike's not very good at lifting people up—at least not physically."

Walking away, I imagined the stars, the planets, and the people I knew aligning to put the play, the school, and San Ramos back together again, and that's when it hit me. I had a plan for making enough money so we could rent a place and do the show off campus, if we could find the right place to rehearse and perform.

## Chapter 18

Tuesday, October 22

San Ramos

I stopped in the greenbelt to text Ms. G. **Got an idea for raising co-curricular funds. You have time to hear it?** She was good about answering quickly, and I wanted her input.

I texted Nicole asking, **How's everything?** If she was ready to plunge back in, I'd asked her to help. Next, I googled Grover's Corners, New Hampshire, the setting for *Our Town*. It was an imaginary place, based on Peterborough, New Hampshire, where the author, Thornton Wilder spent his summers. I spotted a link to an article published in North Andover, which was mentioned in the play. It talked about "short spurts of earthquakes that startled and later terrified a lot of the residents." Perfect. That connection pulled everything together and the show would have a connection to our local disaster.

"For several seconds, there was a deep, powerful deafening rolling that shook the house... I felt that power that leaves you stunned and helpless, reminiscent of my previous experience." We could use that quote from North Andover's Eagle Tribune in the program. A "power that leaves you stunned and helpless." How familiar was that? Stunned on the ladder. Helpless with the campus closed. For all I knew Pete, Jenn, Diego, and Nicole felt as helpless as I did, even if we all had different reasons.

Spike and I crossed the greenbelt, headed for the path that

would take us to Sycamore. Two toddlers in tiny hoodies and jeans were at the swings with their mom. One of then screamed, "Doggie. Doggie." She tried to climb out of the toddler swing, while I locked Spike's leash before he could race over and lick her with mad passion.

"No, girls. He's not our dog," the well-dressed Mom said, pushing the little girl back into her seat.

"He's friendly," I said.

"So is she. Probably too friendly for a strange dalmatian. And too little."

"Understood." He was a big guy, who'd never had toddlers grabbing his fur. We passed the empty basketball courts.

Life would go on, and if I ever had little girls, they would never meet their Uncle Bri, though I'd tell them he'd died a hero. Bri believed in moving forward, so after a moment, I let my thoughts return to a new version of the show I was conjuring up.

We needed an uplifting theme, something to unite us. Spike stopped to sniff some pyracantha bushes. A quail tottered, drunk on the orange berries. There's no law against drunk flying if you're a bird.

"Come, Spike," I said after he left his mark. Could Pete or Diego help me think of a theme? Would resilience work? That was something we all had in common.

We'd print tickets and ask for additional donations at the door, and post a sign saying, "Your donations will help fund the co-curricular activities that are such an important part of the lives of San Ramos High students." We'd perform scenes and songs that showed resilience. No earthquake was going to defeat us.

My phone buzzed. I leaned against an honest-to-goodness white picket fence to read Nicole's text. **Doing okay. No word about Dad. Babysitting. What's up?**

I wrote back, **I've got a fabulous idea. Call when you're free.**

K. Her brothers were hyper, so she used a ton of energy whenever she babysat. She'd be relieved to help me.

Spike and I watched the wind bending Mom's camellia bushes as we approached our darkened house. The bushes bowed deeply, and the few petals still attached in late October clung to their stalks. Looking up at the cloudless blue sky, I whispered, "Bri, can you help me figure this out?"

I listened closely in case he answered. Maybe his words had never been more than wishful thinking, but he used to tell me I could handle anything. Some days he had more faith in me than I had in myself. "I need you, Bri. Everything's so messed up right now. What would a student council leader like you do if you were putting together a show to raise money for activities?"

As I said the words out loud, I knew the answer.

He'd ask everybody he knew to get involved: actors, designers, techies, publicists, and ushers. He'd ask each one to bring ten people to help. He'd find the biggest venue available and have a ticket sales competition to fill it. He'd ask every reporter who covered local high schools or human-interest stories to write about it—or he'd delegate someone to do it. He'd comp reviewers. And he'd ask the Drama Boosters to fund the venue so every dollar we made could help the cause. He might not know how to do all those things, but he'd ask questions. He'd ask for help. That's what a leader does.

"Spike, I know how to do this! Scenes from *Our Town*. Improvs from drama class. Songs from the talent show. And maybe a medley from the whole cast at the end. This will be like the talent show on steroids."

I pulled up Ms. G's last text to the whole cast and wrote, **Want to raise money for activities? I have an idea, but I need help. Be at my house tonight at eight, and I'll tell you about it. Text back if you'll be there.** I read it to Spike before I hit send. He was the closest thing I had to Bri, and maybe it was silly, but I wanted to include both of them.

Next, I asked Nicole to find passages in her monologues that would show Grover's Corners overcoming difficulties. Then I asked Jenn to come up with some songs with lyrics about hope and resilience. Of course she'd ask why, so I told her I wanted an "overcoming earthquakes" playlist. There was no point in getting her all excited if nothing came of this idea, and I didn't want her knowing about it ahead of everyone else.

That evening after the sun sank behind the ridge, I fed Spike and opened my messages before getting ready for the cast to arrive. Ms. G asked about my idea, and I told her I wanted to put together scenes and songs to raise money so drama and music wouldn't die. **Do you want to help? Could we use either theatre?**

**Very enterprising, Sandee. I'll ask Dr. Henderson about the theatre, but he's awfully busy these days. I sure miss all of you.** All of us. For once I belonged. She was the first adult who hadn't said I was too young to help, and I loved the way she respected her students.

If school were in session, I'd store the props before heading to Dad's office to give him a ride home. The car! It was still stuck at the Oakland Airport. "Hey, Siri," I asked, "are there any road closures between San Ramos and the Oakland Airport?"

"Here's what I found," Siri said in a voice that seemed too upbeat to be artificial intelligence.

I clicked on the link, which showed that all the roads had re-opened. "What's wrong with me? Why don't I BART over and pick it up?" I asked Spike since no one else was around. BART had been back in business for almost a week.

Spike cocked his head, made eye contact, and barked.

"Oops! I can't do it tonight if the cast is coming to my meeting."

"Woof!"

"Why am I talking to a dog that only says woof?"

"Woof!"

My phone went off, alerting me to messages rolling in one after another. All were from cast members asking about my idea for raising money. Though it wasn't fully formed, I couldn't wait to share it. What I didn't know I could figure out later. *We* could figure out later.

Be here at eight and bring a flashlight. The power in this town is unstable, I texted.

Isn't that why we left Jenn's last Friday?

When did we meet at Jenn's? another one texted.

Yeah! I wasn't there.

Is *Our Town* happening?

When can we get back on campus?

Be at 617 Sycamore Lane in one hour and I'll tell you all about it.

Amber and Jenn both left messages that said, You rock, Sandee. I loved it. Maria said, Be there if I can get a ride.

I needed to tell my parents that we were going to have a house full of kids for a meeting—not a party. Where were they anyway? Not that it mattered as long as they didn't get caught the way Nicole's dad did.

I sent the text to Mom's phone and checked the refrigerator to make sure we had soft drinks and water. We were going to bring the school some money whether the earthquakes were over or not.

# Chapter 19

## Tuesday, October 22

### The Mason's Living Room

At eight, our doorbell rang. When I opened the door, most of the cast poured into our living room in one big group. "Can we see what's in the fridge?" Tony asked.

"Why don't you grab a water or a Coke from the table and have a seat?"

"Come on, Ed. Let's look in the refrigerator," Tony said as if I hadn't spoken.

As everyone settled on couches, chairs, and the floor, our living room turned into a party minus the beer, joints, and sexy clothes. Instead of talking with each other, though, people kept asking me questions.

"What's your big solution?" Tony said as he settled on the floor.

"How can we do this without a theatre?" Bradley asked, "and is this about doing the show or raising money?"

Before I could answer, Naomi, who headed up the costume crew, said, "If anyone drops out, can I have their part?"

"If we can't do it on campus, who's in charge?"

"How much money are we gonna charge for tickets and who keeps track of it?"

I held up my hand, asking for quiet, and said exactly what

Ms. G did at the beginning of every read through. "I'll answer all your questions in time. First though, I want to set up a few ground rules."

Over everybody's groans and moans somebody said, "Who made you the boss?"

"I hope everybody will work as a team, and I certainly want your input. Ms. G would give us an update on the clean-up effort if she were here, but she may not know any more than we do."

"So, what's your plan?" Bradley asked. He'd taken over my dad's recliner and he'd take over this meeting too, if he thought he could add it to the leadership portion of his resume.

"Right now we need to fund our own activities, right?" I said.

Those who weren't looking at a phone nodded, except Bradley, who tapped his fingers on the arm of Dad's chair.

"We'll be putting on a show about hope, strength, and resilience because those are the things pulling us through this. We're going to use a few of the Stage Manager's monologues from *Our Town*."

"Why?" asked Tony.

"Because the lines relate to living through troubles. We'll include a few scenes from Act One, so this can be like a teaser for when we do the show." Maria nodded, looking up with big brown eyes like her cousin's. Would Diego say I was being a leader or being bossy? And why was I thinking about him right now? "We're going to supplement with a few songs from last spring's talent show."

"Why?" Tony asked again.

"So it will run longer than twenty minutes." Everybody laughed, even Tony and his buddy, Ed, who played a drunken misfit named Simon Stimpson in *Our Town*.

"But where can we rehearse?" Amber asked.

"I thought about having us rehearse in the park, but we need a place that's more private, and the schools and libraries aren't available."

Suddenly, everyone was talking at once again.

"How about a church?"

"How about the Women's Club?"

"How about the Sycamore Clubhouse?"

"How about the Children's Theatre?"

"I could ask all of them and see who'll give us the best deal," Pete said. When did he come in? He wasn't part of the cast, but here he was, volunteering, despite what I'd said to him when he rescued me earlier. He'd be perfect for the job.

"That's a great idea," Jenn said. She stared for another minute, and a sexy smile lit up her face as she looked Pete over. "Who are you?" That girl couldn't stop flirting even in the middle of a crisis.

"The name's Pete. I'm a friend of Sandee's, and I'm here to help."

"We can use *everybody's* help, right?" I didn't look at Jenn as I spoke, but she got the message. "After all, this is for the whole community as well as the school." I'd moved to the brick step in front of the fireplace. Standing there made me three inches taller.

"I thought we were doing this to raise money," Bradley reminded me.

"That too. Resuming normal activities makes this a win-win."

Bradley nodded and Amber, who was watching him, joined in.

Then I heard a familiar voice ask, "Is this meeting for

students only, or can anyone join it?"

"Ms. G! When did you get here?"

"A couple minutes ago. Your text about the meeting came to everyone on the list. The door was open, and you'd already started your meeting, so I've been listening," Ms. G said as she looked at the cast.

"It's great to have you here," I said. "Bradley, give her your seat."

He got up without suggesting a better plan and smiled when she said, "Thank you, Bradley. May I bring everyone up to date on a couple of things?"

"Please," I said, grabbing two bottles of water—one for her and one for me. My throat had gone dry.

"Both scientists and the state government are puzzled by the relationship between the winds, the original quake and the aftershocks," Ms. G, began. "We're in new territory. No one knows if these conditions are the result of climate change, global warming, or something more bizarre. People haven't believed there was a connection between winds and earthquakes since the time of the ancient Greeks, but scientists are reconsidering the possibility. The county and state are waiting for the situation to stabilize before they release any funds."

Maria raised her hand as if we were in school instead of my living room, "What if they can't make all this global warming stuff stop?" I looked at Ms. G and she looked at me.

"Well?" Tony asked. "I heard we're running out of time to fix it."

I didn't think anybody had an answer for him, but Ms. G said, "If we run out of time, we'll learn something new about the consequences of climate change." It wasn't an answer, but I think she was saying that we'd adapt. What choice did we have?

"Sandee, I'm proud of you for trying to get our town back to normal. Now, how can I help?"

"We need to find a performance date. Once we have that and a place to perform, Nicole, Amber, and Bradley can invite the singers from the talent show that we want to participate."

"Why do you want to bring them back?" Jenn said.

"We want to reach out to as many people as possible. Maybe their friends will come to the show." Jenn's lower lip protruded as she stared at my mom's throw rugs.

"Don't we need to get all the activities running again?" Maria asked.

Bradley cut her off. "We need to get back to classes if I'm going to get into Princeton. I need top-notch semester grades and so do a lot of other seniors."

"We can't do anything about our classes." Everyone turned to me when I said that. "It's not within our control, just like the earthquakes and winds. What we can do is make a little money so our activities can go on. Now, who wants to work with Pete and find the perfect venue?"

"That's okay," Pete shouted from the back of the room. "I can handle it on my own."

I sighed without meaning to. Six months ago, when we were doing *Oklahoma!* I'd had the same attitude. I was wrong and so was Pete. Theatre is a group effort. Even if you're doing a one-woman show, you need a director, lights, and probably props. And if you don't have an audience, what's the point? Pete didn't know because he hadn't worked on another show. Or maybe he had and hadn't told me about it. I really didn't know anything about him except that he was a cute loner who could be a Prince Charming when he wanted to. I shook my head and said, "This is a group effort. Who wants to work with Pete?"

Amber and Jenn put up their hands at the same time. Everybody laughed, because they were gorgeous and Pete was handsome, and a whole new drama might be taking shape before their eyes.

"Great," I said, ignoring the potential clashes and jealousies among these beautiful people. "Remember we can rehearse in one place and perform in another."

"We know, Sandee," Pete said. "Come on, girls. Let's go talk on the porch." All three of them were outside in a flash, and the air seemed lighter once both Jenn and Pete were out of the room.

Ms. G said, "If possible, you should perform the weekend before Thanksgiving. That's when everybody expects to see our fall production. Encourage people to donate cash, services, or whatever will help." That reminded me that Mr. Garcia had volunteered to assist, but before I could speak, she said, "Even though this isn't a school activity any more, I'm happy to help sell tickets."

"That would be great, but I'm sure you can help us with a lot more. Since none of us have school…"

She held up a hand to stop me. "I have school, Sandee. Every teacher is scrubbing classrooms or re-shelving books or sweeping up broken glass or tangling with county and state offices.

"You're doing scut work?" Bradley asked. This time nobody laughed.

"We're doing everything we can to reopen school. Professionals will deal with the chemical spills and the debris from the buildings that are gone. We're clearing space for them because it saves the district money."

"We'd love your help any time you're available, Ms. G. I've asked Nicole to find some speeches from *Our Town* that relate to hope."

"Where is she?" Ms. G asked.

Good question. She never missed anything related to a performance, but she wasn't in the room. How I hoped news about her dad wasn't keeping her away.

People were restless, and we'd covered what we needed to, so I thanked the cast for coming. "And before you go," I said as they gathered up back packs and jackets, please sign up for the jobs you can do on the pad of yellow paper by the front door. It's not a contract. I just need to know who's available."

Bradley, Jenn, and Ms. G put our furniture back while I texted Nicole. **Missed you at the meeting. Everything okay?**

I read it out loud before I asked, "Should I say anything else?"

"Why does she get special treatment?" Bradley said.

Apparently, he hadn't heard that Nicole's father was missing. "If she doesn't answer, I'm going over there," I said.

"Want me to go with you?" Bradley said.

"How well do you know her?" Bradley shrugged. Maybe he couldn't see why that mattered.

"It's nice of you to offer, but I'm going alone. There's no reason to overwhelm her if she's gotten bad news."

"Bad news?"

"Her dad's missing," I said without looking up from my phone. She was a private person facing a life-altering crisis, and Bradley barely knew her. She needed a supportive friend instead of a helicopter mom. Besides, I owed her. Bradley probably didn't know about her drunk driving, and I wasn't about to tell him. If her dad had been found ... I remembered the day we heard about Bri. She needed someone who'd been there.

She texted back, **Sorry. Not available today.**

**Everything okay?** I texted again.

When she didn't answer, I texted my parents instead. **Worried about Nicole. Going by her house. Back by ten.** It showed them how responsible I could be even though they weren't home.

As soon as the house was empty, I grabbed the keys, walked into the garage, and saw nothing but empty space. Mom and Dad were using the car. Our only car right now. At least Nicole wasn't expecting me. I reached for my phone to call Pete, but he didn't have a car. Bradley did though. Too bad I'd just said he couldn't come. "I changed my mind, but you have to stay in the car," wouldn't work. Besides, he and Amber showed up together, and I didn't want to interrupt whatever they were doing on the way home.

While I scanned the cast list for someone who could give me a ride, the garage door's motor began whirring. My heart pounded as it rose. I stepped back and saw two pairs of headlights.

What now? Who had swiped our garage door opener and what were they planning to steal? I started to call 9-1-1, but the Volvo horn beeped loudly. Looking again, I saw Dad's headlights behind Mom's. Apparently, they'd gone to Oakland in her car and picked up the Camry.

"Perfect timing," I said as he opened the driver's door." Can I borrow your car, Dad? Nicole's not answering her phone, and…"

"Maybe she's sleeping?"

"Can I please make sure? It's really important."

He looked at Mom, who nodded. "Be back in less than an hour." Looking at his cell he added, "I'm setting a timer."

Dad put his keys in my hand, and I said, "Thanks for trusting me. I just need to check because of her dad."

"We know," Mom said quietly. "You're a good friend but stay safe." I nodded as I got into the Camry. No one knew when the earth might start shaking again. Worse still, it could open into gaping holes like they now had in Hayward and San Leandro. The pictures on the news made me grateful to live in dull old San Ramos.

The porch light was off at Nicole's house, which meant they hadn't gone out. Only her brothers would be in bed at nine forty-five, so I called Nicole again. Got the "leave a message" message. She was incommunicado. I love the sound of that word. So lyrical and private. This time, though, I was afraid it meant trouble.

I got out of the car anyway, because I had to know she was okay. The doorbell chimed loudly. If no one answered... Muffled footsteps interrupted my thought. Nicole's whispered, "Who is it?"

"Sandee Mason. You okay?"

"I'm fine. I'll talk to you tomorrow."

"Did you get bad news?"

"I'll talk to you tomorrow," she repeated without answering my question. I hate it when people do that. It takes two to make a friendship, but only one to put up a wall. Knowing Nicole, she'd put a door in that wall as soon as she was ready, but when people decide they need space they usually need a reliable person to listen instead. I hoped she knew support was available. She didn't deserve her mother's distrust.

I couldn't slow down my thoughts, and I certainly wasn't ready to go home. Circling through town, I saw couples at restaurants on the south end where the earthquake wasn't as bad. Outside of Starbucks, workers stacked chairs. The cracked glass in their windows had been replaced. Pete wasn't sitting outside. Maybe he was with Jenn? The thought made my stomach curdle, though maybe they deserved each other.

Before I went by Starbucks, I'd passed evidence of the disaster. Luigi's Pizza, the deli, Kubler's, the burned-out Rivera restaurant, and every entrance to San Ramos High was covered with caution tape that already looked old and battered.

Three temporary floodlights shone on the remains of the science and art wings. They stood like dollhouses, open on one side with their interiors exposed, like a bomb had exploded, ripping equipment and books to shreds. Dumpsters surrounded what was left. Their enemy had been a natural phenomenon rather than bombs, but this felt like war.

I parked across the street and stared into the chaotic mess. Why had nature ganged up on us? Was it deliberate or justified or a fate beyond our understanding?

Tessa popped into my mind as I sat staring at the war zone that used to be our school. She'd know exactly what to say if Nicole's father were in the hospital or worse. She'd had experience because of the brain injury her sister experienced in Afghanistan. Nobody knew when or if she'd regain consciousness. Thinking about her, and the dark October night pressing up against the car, heaviness came over me. The world was weighing me down, and the air was oppressively thick on my skin.

When my phone rang, I jumped. The screen said Amber. Guess she got my number from one of Ms. G's mass texts. "Hi, Sandee. Pete's misplaced his phone, but he wanted to talk to you."

"Hey, kiddo, do you have a blurb about San Ramos drama? It'd help people see how legit we are."

"A blurb? What was he talking about? I've got programs from last year's season, and the drama department has a page on the school's website."

"URL please?" he asked.

"www.Sanramoshigh.edu."

"That's what Amber showed me," Pete said. "Got anything else?"

"Like I said, I can loan you copies of the programs from *Oklahoma!* and the talent show."

"Right. How about if I come by tomorrow morning and pick them up?"

"Okay."

"Around nine? Is that good for you?" No kidding around. No flirting. When did he get so business-like?

"I guess so. It's not like I can give them to you at school."

"Funny." When I didn't say anything more he added, "Hey, thanks. Together we're going to pull this off."

I'd said the same thing less than an hour ago. Good thing the sentiment was catching on. "Get home safely," I added, even though I hadn't seen where his home was.

"Sure." I imagined him handing the phone back to Amber. Maybe she'd help Pete get a little more responsible or less evasive. I couldn't pinpoint the problem, which was weird since I was usually great at separating the popular kids from the jocks, the drifters from the brains, and the druggies from the goths. He didn't fit into any category—not even drifters or brain.

Most seniors were driven or defiant, but not Pete. Maybe if Amber and he worked together, he'd drop some of his mystique. Or maybe our whole relationship wasn't meant to be.

Too many maybes right now. As I headed home, the clock on the GPS said 10:38. I was about to call my parents when I remembered that they assumed I was with Nicole. Since they hadn't called me, things were cool, and I shouldn't disturb them. Maybe if I let go, they'd trust me more.

## Chapter 20

### Wednesday, October 23

### Sandee's House

The next morning, stripes of sunshine covered my blanket. The way they alternated between light and dark reminded me of the mood swings everyone slipped into these days. I peeked at my phone, and saw it was already eight-thirty, and I had a text from Jenn. **Hope Songs: "I Hope You Dance," "Wind Beneath My Wings," "We Are Family," "Stronger (What Doesn't Kill You)," "Give Us Hope," and "Be Okay." Will these work?**

Admittedly, I didn't give her a specific number, but five songs weren't much to work with. "Give Us Hope" was a fave, and "Wind Beneath My Wings" always stirred something inside me. So what if that made me a geek or a nerd or both?

If we were going to have people sing, we needed a choir director. Mr. Jackson's house over in Oakland suffered some serious damage, and he'd taken a leave for the rest of the semester to repair it. Nicole would be an excellent singing coach if she weren't so worried about her dad. Besides, she was already busy putting the Stage Manager's speeches together. Okay. I didn't know many of the seniors, but there had to be someone who was qualified. I'd talk to Nicole, and we'd figure it out.

Standing by my window, I saw the Rivera's lawn looking shaggy. *Somebody will care for you again,* I wanted to tell it.

Someone will trim your hedges. I wasn't really talking to the lawn, of course. I miss Diego's companionship, his promising kiss before he left, and the potential our lives used to have.

Jenn's text was waiting, so I put **Good job. Got any suggestions for singers?** It was more diplomatic than asking if she'd left off half her list.

**Let me think**, she texted back, which was an improvement over her usual airheaded comments.

I needed more songs, so I texted Bradley. **Know any songs about hope or resilience for our show? Help us plan and you can put it on your resume as a leadership skill.** Bradley never turned down a chance to build his resume. I looked at my cell and realized it was time to throw on clothes. Pete would be here in fifteen minutes.

Once I'd dressed, I stole into Bri's room, hoping Mom wouldn't ask what I was doing. It still smelled of old socks and aftershave. I'd stored the programs in Bri's desk. It seemed right to keep them there, after Rob got drunk last spring right before our final dress rehearsal of *Oklahoma!* and I wound up getting him out of the park and then almost got arrested for driving with a permit instead of a license. I thought Bri'd like seeing the program from the show I wound up stage-managing. Of course, he could have seen it in my room... if he could see at all. Losing someone you've known all your life makes you think crazy things sometimes.

Though Mom dusted and vacuumed his room every week, I didn't think she'd been in the drawer because both programs were right where I'd left them. "Got to borrow these, Bri," I whispered. "It's important."

I was on my way out when I realized Bri's room would make an awesome rehearsal studio. All we needed to do was move the bed and his footlocker over to the wall. If we could use Bri's room for rehearsal, we'd only need a place to perform.

The awkward part was that Mom would have to stop treating Bri's room like a shrine, and I didn't know if she could. Bri wouldn't care. If he knew, he might even be happy about it. Maybe people on the other side wanted the living to move on.

I heard the doorbell, called out, "I'll get it, Mom," and raced down the stairs, programs in hand. The whole committee stood in front of me dressed in what adults call business casual. "Wow. This is great! Can I take a picture?"

"Okay with you two?" Pete asked, throwing an arm around each of them. Amber and Jenn nodded like a couple of bobble-head dolls. Maybe I was a little jealous, because I'd thrown on yesterday's clothes, and they looked mature and classy as they posed. All three admired the photo, complete with autumn leaves and a cerulean sky, courtesy of our ongoing windstorms. "You want to role play what you'll say?" I asked. When they stared blankly, I added, "Like an improv?"

Pete shook his head. "You've got three excellent people on this. Trust us, Sandee."

"You're doing your job. Let us do ours," Jenn added. I couldn't believe how much she sounded like Pete. Maybe being able to absorb other people's personalities made her a good actress.

"Performances will be on the $21^{st}$, $22^{nd}$ and $23^{rd}$ of November with a dress rehearsal on the $20^{th}$, right?" Pete said.

"Exactly."

"And you'll give credit in the program to anyone who lets us use their space?" Jenn asked.

"Of course." I hadn't even thought about the program, but I'd done one for *Oklahoma!* and another for last spring's talent show, so it made sense for me to handle it.

"And give us program credit for finding the venue?" Amber said, trying out the role of a saleswoman who negotiated. She'd always been reserved when she wasn't on stage, and I liked this new side of her.

"Sure. I just hope the acknowledgements won't be longer than the program. If they need any information about what we can pay for rentals, have them contact Ms. G. She'll talk to the Drama Boosters."

"We've got it, worry woman," Pete said.

"Will you send me a copy of that picture you took?" Jenn asked. "I want to post it on Instagram and TikTok."

"Absolutely. Tell everybody what you're working on." I clicked and it whooshed out of my cell phone and over to hers.

As Amber's car pulled out of the driveway, I realized I didn't know where they were going. Sighing, I told myself it would be okay. Pete wouldn't screw this up. He wasn't going to let himself look foolish in front of two genuine foxy chicks. Besides if he made a mistake, we'd fix it together. I wasn't in this alone.

Later, I went into messages and found Bradley's list of hope songs. Jenn and he both recommended "Give Us Hope" and "Wind Beneath My Wings", which were my faves. He also listed "One Day at a Time", which was odd because we're in a very different kind of recovery. Had he heard the lyrics, which were about recovering from drugs and alcohol, or was he including it for its upbeat tune? He made up for his weird choice with "Here Comes the Sun," a Beatles classic. Vintage! It would appeal to the parents and grandparents in the audience. How cool would it be to have our teachers join in as we sang that one? I could imagine it as a finale, bringing us all together. If everyone joined in, would that be too sentimental? How did directors and producers make all these decisions?

Going back upstairs, past the pictures of my Girl Scout days and Bri's student council events, I made a mental list of our acts.

Opening: Short speech telling why we're doing this.

Act One: Scenes from *Our Town*. Begin and end with Nicole. Include:

o breakfast scene at the Gibbs house

o homework scene with George and Emily

o maybe the soda fountain scene from Act Two

o the Stage Manager talking about the importance of family and overcoming difficulties.

Intermission Music.

Second Act Opening: "Wind Beneath My Wings?"

Act Two: Alternate

o scenes

o monologues

o improvs

o songs.

I pulled up the program from last spring's talent show on my computer. "Wind Beneath My Wings" had closed Act One. This time it could open Act II. Tessa, who'd been one of the singers, would love to be a part of this. She was always up for good causes, and, knowing her, she'd bring in a whole new audience of college kids. She might even know where her duet partner was now.

The San Ramos High Improv Troupe could handle anything an audience threw at them, and they'd take morbid suggestions and turn them into something funny. The performers could ask questions like "May I have a suggestion of an object that might disappear during an earthquake?" "May I have an emotion you felt after the big one?" "May I have a suggestion of something that could fall off a shelf in an aftershock?" That would tie the improvs into our theme and purpose.

We'd add only two or three scenes from plays and musicals—maybe *Blithe Spirit*, *Mean Girls*, and something else. I'd ask Nicole, Bradley, and Amber for ideas—plus Jenn, since she couldn't be left out of anything. With four or five improvs, plus a few songs, we'd have around twelve short pieces. At three minutes a piece that would be thirty-six minutes, plus a minute for each scene change would take us to forty-eight minutes. Or forty-five minutes if the scene changes went quickly.

This show would rock. The school missed out when they refused to let us help them clean up the place and get the place ready for classes. Why didn't adults trust kids, instead of making us prove ourselves?

## Chapter 21

### Wednesday, October 23

### Later That Day at Sandee's House

Tessa called me at four-thirty. "I tracked down Taylor Gray. You remember her?"

"Short black hair. She sang 'Wind Beneath My Wings' with you?"

"Exactly!"

"Facebook, Twitter, or Instagram?"

"Friend of a friend. She's at UC Berkeley, and she'd love to reprise the song."

"Terrific!" I wiggled my toes, which is how I do a happy dance when I'm on the phone.

"Taylor suggested we dedicate our song to the people who'd lost their lives in the earthquake. What do you think?"

"Sure," I thought of Nicole's dad and glanced through the window at Diego's yard. There were all kinds of losses to memorialize. "It's a great idea. We're going to rehearse at my house and maybe a couple of other places."

"Thanks, but we can rehearse on our own," Tessa said. "I still have the tape we used to get ready for the talent show."

"Wonderful, because I forgot to tell you that you might need your own accompaniment."

There was a pause, and I heard a big sigh before she asked,

"Don't you have someone who's playing the piano for the other acts?"

"Not yet. I'm going to ask Mr. Jackson if he has any suggestions."

"Could he do it himself?" Tessa said. "He was always real supportive."

"I don't think he'd leave Oakland right now. The big one went under his house and he's trying to rebuild the thing. I hope he doesn't hurt his hands."

"At least give him a call," she said. "Maybe he knows someone who could fill in."

"I sure will. Can I switch subjects on you?" I asked walking back to my desk, which was dotted with layers of post-its. "It's about Nicole." I'd gotten a message from her earlier. She'd picked three speeches, but she couldn't concentrate.

In a tense voice Tessa asked, "What happened?"

"We don't know. Her dad's been missing since the earthquake, and the police found his jacket and wallet in a trash can on 12th Street in downtown Oakland. That's got to be fifteen miles, and I can't imagine he walked it, which adds layers of new possibilities. Plus there was no cell phone, so her mom tried his number one more time, and …" I gulped, trying not to choke on my own words. "…and a total stranger answered. He said the number was new to him and hung up. I have no idea how to help."

Tessa said, "That poor girl has gone through enough."

She was right. My throat swelled. Losses surrounded us, but if Nicole quit the show, we'd all lose. Life wasn't fair, and when I thought about Nicole, the show was the least of my worries. What would happen if my dad or mom disappeared? Staring at the floral rug on my hardwood floor, I said, "If you were me, what would you say?"

"Do you remember what I said when you found out about Bri?"

I swung around in my desk chair, trying to recall that awful day. "Not really. All I remember is that you made me feel better."

"Do the same thing for her. She's not going to remember any more than you do. Let her know you're there for her. Remind her that doing the show will help take her mind off the uncertainty. If you think it's appropriate, ask if her father would expect her to keep going."

"Yes! You asked me if Bri wouldn't want me to do that."

"Impressive memory. Now you're paying it forward. I'm proud of you."

"Thanks for helping me figure it out, Tessa."

"No problem. Call me when you know where you're going to perform, okay?"

"Absolutely. I should put you on the group text."

"No, Sandee. I'm on enough lists already. Don't put me on until the last possible moment, okay?"

"Sure."

We hung up, and I wrote her suggestions on the nearest post-it pad. I was still writing when my phone vibrated against the desk's surface. Pete texted Found a big hall at the local Episcopal Church. They do a musical here every year. They're donating space to SRHS for the 19th through the 23rd of November. Extra night.

Great! Thanks, Pete, I texted back.

They'll put a notice in their weekly bulletin explaining we're raising money. Maybe some of their congregation will pitch, Pete wrote back.

I sent him a smiley face emoji. Maybe he was becoming as dependable as Diego but that didn't make me feel any less hassled.

And they'll let us sell cookies and bottled water at intermission to raise more if we want to. They asked who was in charge, and I told them the drama teacher cuz they need someone over eighteen to sign the contract, he added.

Good. I was fine with Ms. G being the adult in charge. She said she'd help any way she could. How did you talk them into it?

Google said they do community outreach. Their goals matched ours.

So I texted WTG! Do you think you could match one of my goals? I swiveled in my chair, so my back was to the window looking at the Rivera's front yard. Right now, I wasn't comfortable thinking about Diego.

Probably.

I want to see your place. Why won't you let me do that?

Come by any time. Let me know when you're on your way and I'll text you my address. He said it glibly but if I did it, I figured he wouldn't be home or he wouldn't answer. He could be such a cool guy when he wanted to. Clearly Jenn and Amber trusted him, but I suspected I knew him better.

Of course, Diego knew me for almost a year before he invited me inside his house even though he lived next door. He'd been to my place, like Pete, and he kept telling me it wasn't a good time for me to come over. Once we spent an afternoon in his family room, working together on a social studies project, we both wondered what he'd been afraid of.

This was different. Pete was a senior and such a good-looking guy. My heart jumped when I looked at the screen on my phone and saw he'd texted again. A bunch of us are going over to Starbucks. Come join us?

**Jenn's coming over for dinner.** As soon as I read it, I hit delete. Pete would get us sidetracked. Besides, if he decided to flirt with Jenn, Dad would get defensive, and I'd be tongue-tied. He wanted me to like Pete as much as I wanted to use Bri's room for rehearsal. Pete was cute and foxy, but he was also a heartbreak looking for a place to land. How many times had he built me up, only to turn around and ignore me?

**Can't**, I texted. Maybe he'd see what messages without explanations felt like. If he wanted to say anything, the door was wide open. I had more to do, like texting Mr. Jackson and making sure we were having something decent for dinner. Since Jenn was going to help me convince Mom and Dad that Bri would want us to use his room, she deserved the kind of healthy food she liked.

Dinner was ready at six-thirty when Jenn arrived in her skinny jeans and a sweater with swirls of fall colors. After we sat down Mom said, "I'm glad you came by Jenn. What's happening with your parents' theatre?" Amazing. Mom set the stage for a conversation she couldn't possibly be anticipating.

"The theatre wasn't damaged, so my parents are still offering classes for kids and planning a Christmas show."

"Which one?" It was an odd question for Mom, who knew nothing about children's theatre.

"'No Time for Christmas.' Have you heard of it?" Jenn asked, picking at the meat loaf Mom made from scratch. If she was a vegetarian again this week, she could eat the broccoli and the boiled potatoes.

"I think Bri might have been in a play with that title in about third grade." Mom was now staring at her meatloaf so intently that I glanced at mine. Normal meatloaf. Did she somehow know what I was about to ask?

"Mom, guess what?" She looked at me without saying anything. "Jenn, Amber, and Pete found a performance space. All we need is a place to rehearse."

"Actually, we need a lot of places to rehearse, Mrs. Mason," Jenn said, "and our theatre is being used for the Christmas play, so I suggested maybe we could use some garages."

I stared because I had suggested it, not Jenn. She caught on and gave me a look that said trust me. "We don't have any bands, so we won't disturb the neighbors, and we'd rehearse in the daytime since there's no school. Most of your neighbors would be at work."

Quickly I swallowed my food and said, "It'd really help the cause. Like Jenn said, we need lots of spaces because the show goes up in November."

I took a sip of my water. Every time I was around Jenn or Nicole, I opted for water over soda. At first I thought they would respect my choice. Now it didn't matter. I did it because diet soda pop had a funny aftertaste. I didn't miss the chemicals or carbonation any more than I missed my daily package of share size M&Ms. Sometimes a small package now lasted three days or longer.

"Did you know that all performers work better when they're in front of an audience? It makes a huge difference to have people watching," Jenn asked. She'd finished her broccoli and I passed her the bowl. I hadn't given up all my bad habits, and I was saving room because Mom had a plate of brownies in the kitchen. It would be rude not to eat at least one.

Mom turned to Dad and said, "What do you think, Tom?"

"Sounds like a good cause, but we can't just turn over the garage without knowing who's going to use it."

"We don't have anybody flaky in the show. Besides, I'll be

here, and I won't let anybody walk away with your tools or anything." He didn't have a lot of tools anyway, so why was he concerned? I gave him a big smile that said trust me.

"Let's give it a try. Let us know who's rehearsing, though, okay?" Dad said.

"Sure," Jenn and I said together. She added, "Bradley and Amber have offered their garages too, but when I asked Pete about his he never answered. Could you ask him, Sandee? After all, you're the stage manager."

"He didn't take you by his place, did he?" I asked. She shook her head. "I'll ask, but I wouldn't count on it." I wasn't saying anything else in front of Mom and Dad. Jenn shrugged. She had parents of her own to deal with.

Mom brought the brownies in from the kitchen. Seeing them made me think of Bri because they were his favorites, and I realized that with three garages, we wouldn't need his old bedroom. It was kind of nice to sneak in alone and breathe in the past. Maybe this was the best possible plan. We could set up a schedule and let the performers who needed the most work rotate through all three garages.

Tessa was right when she said she and her partner could work alone. Other singers could too, but actors sometimes bickered if someone wasn't in charge. We rehearsed our scenes for class without a director, and I'd had a couple of flakes for scene partners—one who improvised his lines and one who brought an unopened bottle of Jack Daniels instead of tea for the moment when he offered me a drink. Sometimes I wondered how Ms. G coped with all the uncertainties of doing a show.

## Chapter 22

### Wednesday, October 23

### Sandee's House and Downtown San Ramos

After Jenn left, the wind kicked up again, making me restless. Details about the show churned in my head along with a deep, nagging fear that the big earthquakes might come back.

I needed to get away from the isolation I felt with Diego in Fallon. Spike had been walked, so I couldn't use him as an excuse to go out. Instead I said, "I've got some things to return to the library." My voice sounded too chipper to me, and Dad said, "Haven't they been closed for a while?"

"I'm just going to slide some books into the drop box. I'll be back by ten."

"You'd better take the car," Dad said without even checking his watch. "It's dark out there."

"Perfect."

"Remember to put the seat back...," he said and I joined him as he added, "... and don't leave the gas tank empty."

"You're growing up, Sandee,"

I nodded, knowing that if I said, "It's about time you realized that," he'd get mad. My parents are good people, but they don't always understand that high school has changed since they were kids.

Sitting under a big light in the 7-Eleven lot an hour later, my phone buzzed with a text from Jenn. An earthquake took out a bedroom wall and the dining room of Jackson's house. He can't spare the time to coach singers.

What do we do now? I wrote back.

Maybe my singing coach could do it?

Ask! Okay?

K. Bye, Jenn texted.

It was already nine forty-five—time to either call Dad or go home and show him I was responsible. Stroke his ego. Sometimes you need to do that with parents.

While I filled the gas tank, I noticed a man sitting with his back up against the chain link fence at the edge of the station. This guy wore a grey hoodie tied close around his face and faded jeans and black Reeboks. Once Dad and I drove through Berkeley and he told me people sat around like that when they had no place else to be. I asked what he meant, and he explained they had no home or job. He said they were between addresses.

We'd talked about the homeless last semester in school, but I never understood how they managed. Didn't they need a place to sleep at night and change their clothes and a kitchen to cook food in? As far as I knew, we never had a homeless problem in San Ramos. If the earthquake changed that, no one said so—not that I'd talked to many people since the school closed. Was there caution tape around this guy's home? Wasn't there someone who'd take him in?

I knew better than to walk up to a stranger and ask questions, no matter how badly I wanted to. Instead, after I filled Dad's tank, I drove right by him—maybe 10 feet away—with my window rolled down. He didn't look up. Didn't notice. Didn't hold up a stained cardboard sign saying, "Will work for food."

Maybe he was sleeping. Maybe he was stoned. I'd seen

movies about people on the street getting stoned. It was a dangerous way to escape.

Driving away, I was grateful I had a home to go to. As I turned on my street, the moon cast enough light to make leafy patterns on the sidewalk. I wondered if the Berkeley police were still looking for Nicole's dad and the others who'd been reported missing. Had her mom hired a private detective? Why hadn't Tia Wong or some other newscaster given her some publicity? Nicole would give a great interview.

Breathe, Sandee, I whispered at the stop light. You can't take care of everyone. Go home.

Once I got in the kitchen, I grabbed an apple, told Mom and Dad I was back, and went upstairs to put Nicole and her dad at the top of my list for tomorrow. Yawning, I dimmed the recessed cans overhead and sat in the window seat staring at Diego's house. Spike curled up on the floor beside me, and I listened to Jenn's songs one more time. Hearing "Here Comes the Sun" by the light of a nearly full moon felt weird. Everything was turned upside down and almost nothing meant what it used to. Even so, the song was filled with hope. For the older teachers and the parents, it would bring back memories. What would Ms. G be thinking when she heard it? What would Nicole's mom think? Or my parents?

The wind came in bursts now, often without detectable quakes happening simultaneously. I still checked the USGS site daily, so I knew tremors happened regularly, but they were mostly between 1.5 and 3.5, which were teensy next to the 7.1 that rocked our world.

Dad told me one or two clients called every day with a report about a slow gas leak or a new crack in the walls. Grayco Insurance might lose a lot of money, but that wasn't his fault. So much of this was beyond our control that it doubled my determination to help people. I'd take charge of anything I could.

We couldn't go back to the era when the Beatles wrote "Here Comes the Sun." Who'd want to? No internet. No iPhone. No way! A little nostalgia might be fun for a night though.

A Night of Nostalgia. What a great theme for a Halloween party. It would be perfect for our cast. Come as your character or anyone you'd like to be. Lots of kids partied regularly while school was closed. The videos on social media didn't lie. Nobody gave drama parties any more, now that Rob was gone, and the popular juniors and seniors didn't know I was alive, but everyone in the cast did. Without Diego and school, with Pete's repeated disappearing acts, and Nicole worrying about her dad, I didn't feel like partying unless there was a purpose behind it. This would engage all of us and help us get to know each other. It might even help Nicole smile again.

The whole world was willing to help with a party. Compared to putting on this show, a party would be simple.

## Chapter 23

### Eight days later—October 31

### Sandee Mason's Living Room

Dark jeans, a black turtleneck, and a clipboard were my costume for the Halloween party. That's what a stage manager usually wears, and tonight I felt comfortable showing off the real me. I even tucked the turtleneck into my pants and put on some dark lipstick.

Pete came by earlier to help carve pumpkins. Now their orange faces flickered in the windows. While he was here, I listed a bunch of theatre games we could play, hoping it wasn't too geeky.

"Maybe you should just let everybody talk," he suggested. "Share stories and see where things go."

"Maybe. Sounds practical. What if somebody brings beer?"

He looked at his Reeboks as he said, "No big deal. It's a party."

"But I'd be responsible if anything happened, wouldn't I?"

"I suppose, and your parents would hate it. They aren't going to be here, are they?"

"I got them gift certificates for dinner and a movie."

"Must be nice to be rich."

"I'm not rich. I'm a saver."

He rolled his eyes and changed the subject. "If you don't

want kids drinking, don't let 'em in, but it could be a small party."

A tiny shudder ran through me. I dreaded the consequences if kids drank and somebody got in an accident later. I didn't think I could face the consequences on top of everything else. "I hope your strategy works. Got another question."

"Stop stressing," Pete said. A sexy grin stretched across his face. "Watch a movie or just chill. You've got everything set, and I'll be back at seven to help." He wasn't really a part of the show, but maybe he wanted to be my date. My insides tingled when I thought about it. I hoped Maria wouldn't tell Diego if she ever talked to him.

Pete came early, and when we heard a knock on the door, we answered it together. Bradley (George Gibbs) wore an old Princeton letter sweater with moth holes and Amber (Emily Webb) was in a yellow dress with wide ruffles. She had a huge bow in her hair.

"You think George is going to Princeton?" I asked.

"Maybe. This was my great-great grandfather's sweater, so it's almost the right era."

"Now I know why Princeton is your first choice. It runs in your family."

His grin widened. "Grandpa, then Dad and then Uncle Bill went. Now it's my turn. All the Thorpe sons go to Princeton unless they're losers," he said.

I nodded, turning toward Amber. "You look perfect for Emily."

"It might not be the right color for Ms. G's production, but it'll work for our fundraising show. It's vintage," she said, as if it weren't obvious to anyone looking on it.

"Don't spill on it," Bradley said, nudging her.

They looked at each other and laughed.

"Are you two a couple now?" I asked.

Amber shrugged, but her smile told the story. Bradley grinned, and I knew they were falling in love, whether they said so or not. A year ago, I might not have seen it in their eyes, but I recognized the look now. Love was a huge confidence booster, even though it sometimes got so confusing.

Jenn came dressed in a power suit, which seemed completely out of character until she said, "Since I'm doing so much, I thought this would show that I'm multi-tasking. Besides, I didn't want to wear a dowdy housedress like Mrs. Gibbs would."

"You've outdone yourself," I said as enthusiastically as I could.

Our living room was crammed with kids talking about their costumes and hanging out without homework. Jenn and Maria talked about our new show, and a group obsessed about repairing earthquake damage, lost devices, and things not uploaded to the cloud. As far as I could tell, they were drinking Cokes or Sprites, and I was relieved that nobody'd snuck in a bottle. We had tons of snacks courtesy of the huge party trays Bradley and Amber brought.

As soon as there was a lull in the conversation, Pete asked, "Who can tell us their life story in three minutes or less?"

Nobody volunteered, so he said, "I came; I saw; I conquered."

Bradley said, "I thought that was Caesar's story."

"Okay, smart guy, you're next," Pete said before I got a word in. "Three minutes. Sandee, have you got a timer?"

I held up my phone and said, "Go."

"Born in Westport, Connecticut. Moved to San Ramos when my dad was promoted to VP at Chevron. I play tennis, am on student council, take AP classes, and plan to go to Princeton next year. Maybe someone in this room will join me there," he added, looking at Amber, who turned bright red.

The doorbell rang, and Maria said, "I'll get it."

Tony stumbled in with Ed, who played Simon Stimson, the drunken choir leader in *Our Town*. Tonight he smelled like San Ramos's town drunk. "Sup?" he asked.

"I'll handle this, Maria," I said as she stepped back. "You guys are drunk."

"Yup. 's a party," Tony said before he belched.

"No alcohol, remember?" They looked at each other and burst out laughing. "Go," I insisted.

"Make me, Ms. Big Shot," said Tony. Ed laughed again.

"It's my house."

"Your parents' house, and my first real high school party. Everybody gets drunk in high school."

"Go." I would have closed the door on them, but they'd pushed past me, and they were already in the living room.

Bradley pulled himself away from Amber and asked, "What's going on?"

"They're drunk and uninvited."

"Freshmen," Amber said at the same time Pete stepped up.

Ed held up a six-pack in each hand and asked, "Anybody want some?"

Pete said, "Leave, now, before I get pissed and throw you out. You don't have a clue how stupid you're being."

"We belong as much as you do," Tony said pointing at Pete.

"I said to get out. NOW!" Pete grabbed the front of Tony's shirt and threw him onto the porch.

"I'm going, I'm going," Ed said. From the porch he added, "This isn't over."

Pete said, "Trust me. It's over. He turned away from the door and added, "They're a couple of wimps."

"Should we call somebody?" I asked.

"Not your problem," Bradley said. "I know a lot of people are buzzed when they leave a party but who gets drunk before they even come? They'll realize how stupid they were as soon as they sober up."

"Hope so." Everybody was staring and I quickly said, "Okay, who wants to tell their life story in three minutes or less?"

"I'll give it a try," Jenn said, standing up like a board president in her power suit.

The stories went on until someone asked, "Do you have Netflix or HBO?"

"Sure."

"Let's watch a Halloween movie. Maybe *The Craft*," the props coordinator suggested.

Bradley snorted. "You just want to see some foxy chicks who'd never look at you in real life."

Amber play-punched him in the shoulder as she said, "Don't be rude. How about a classic like *Nightmare on Elm Street* or *Poltergeist*?"

"*Poltergeist* sounds good to me," said Jenn. "Any objections?"

I didn't say anything, though I thought of Bri and his messages. I wasn't expecting anything to happen, but if Halloween is the night the spirits travel between the worlds, I wanted him to understand. It's only a movie, Bri, I said in my head. The movie's made up, but you're real. Were real. I don't know. Can you show me where the earthquakes and wind are taking us? Is it global warming or is it just a weird fall? You can see the big picture, can't you?

Bradley reached for the remote, and Pete offered me a bottle of water. "Can I sit with you Ms. Hostess? You throw a great party." He draped his arm around my shoulders before the first scene of *Poltergeist* was over. I hoped Bri could see me. As I settled in, I wondered how Diego was spending Halloween. I couldn't help it. We'd been too close for too long.

"You're special," Pete whispered in my ear.

"You too," I answered. "Let's watch the movie."

What would Nicole think of *Poltergeist*? I looked around but she wasn't in the room. That's when I realized I hadn't seen her all night... again.

# Chapter 24

## Friday, November 1

### The Mason's Home and Garage

After everyone went home, Pete told me the party had been cool, and he helped me clean the living room. "Your drama friends are the bomb," he said, as he dumped empty Coke cans into a garbage bag.

"You're right. Mind if I switch subjects?" He shrugged.

"Did you take a look at the lights, or mics, or acoustics when you looked at the church hall?" I stared at the sofa cushion. It was easier than looking at him.

"What brought that up? I got you a place to perform. Isn't that enough?"

"You said they do shows there, right?" I asked.

"That's what the secretary told me."

"Okay. I keep worrying about possible problems. No one knows what's going on with the earthquakes. The winds have increased and nobody can tell… Never mind. I'm trying to think of everything, and it's exhausting."

"Chill, Sandee. Nobody expects you to think of everything. Do you think your parents would mind if I slept on the sofa?"

"Probably not. I'll ask."

"Don't wake them up. I've done it before, and I'll slip out so early they won't even have to know."

"Okay. I'm too tired to think."

The next morning, I awoke to soft snuffle-snores. Daylight shone across my blanket in wider strips today since I hadn't shut the blinds tightly. Nobody could see in except the birds in the trees. I hadn't dreamed about the show or last night's party or received any messages from Bri.

Spike, the source of those snuffle-snores, had his nose next to my ear. As I petted his head, I heard Mom and Dad talking downstairs, checked the time, and jumped out of bed. We had twenty minutes until rehearsal. I pawed through my clothing, looking for something that would give me authority. A casual leader. Gray jeans and my butterfly tee would work. Looking out the bedroom window, I saw the wind stirring the few leaves still clinging to the treetops. I threw on a dark green hoodie, pulled on my old Greta Thunberg socks, and slipped into my Nikes. Then I drafted a text.

Hi, Ms. Wong. I'm writing you again about my friend, Nicole's dad. He's been missing since the earthquake. They found his jacket with his empty wallet in it. When Nicole's mom called his phone, a stranger answered. I thought one of your human-interest stories might help the family reunite.

I read it over, then added both Nicole's phone number and mine. My index finger was poised over send when a new thought struck me: What if she got hundreds of these every day? I should add a sentence reminding her who I was. If my note struck a chord, Nicole would be surprised. Make that thrilled. A story on TV was bound to get more people looking for her dad.

As I stood up, my stomach growled. Five minutes later, sitting at the kitchen table with Mom's scrambled eggs in front of me, I remembered there were lots of other channels that did interviews. Lots of podcasts too, and any of them could post Nicole's dad's picture on their website. Once it was there it would stay up awhile. My request to Tia Wong should go out everywhere, and maybe people would repost. "Your eggs were great Mom, but it's almost time for rehearsal."

"Okay. Whatever you need." Mom's monotone worried me. I thought she'd pull out of her new depression, but she kept slipping back into it. "You feel all right?" I asked.

"Go. I'll be okay."

I had to take her at her word. I sent Nicole's story to every location on the list I'd made after the big quake. Had it only happened four weeks ago?

Next, I hurried into the garage to sweep the leaves out, set up for rehearsal, and see if the grease spots needed more kitty litter. Nicole was already waiting outside. "Aunt Nancy came to check on Mom," she said, as I offered her a sip from my juice box. "They were having coffee and yogurt when I left and—get this—Mom was laughing."

"Fabulous. What a difference!" Maybe she wouldn't have chronic depression like my own mom.

With a big grin on her face she said, "Today I can concentrate." She was wearing lipstick and mascara again. Something had shifted, and I was happy for her.

As the actors showed up, I slid from stage manager to director, asking the characters what they wanted, what they could do to get it, and what was in their way. Ms. G always asked those questions, and I helped the actors get specific, which made me feel like an acting coach.

Bradley acted more pompous than George, or maybe he was more self-assured. Sometimes there's a fine line between the two.

Maybe he was showing off for Emily, his girlfriend in the show, or maybe he was showing off for Amber, who played Emily and was wearing a low-cut tee that left little to the imagination. On stage or off, the two of them had a promising chemistry. They'd hold the audience's attention.

Before rehearsal ended, I said, "Can we run the segments so I can time them?"

Tony groaned. I gave him the Bowen look, and he said, "Sorry." Maybe he was embarrassed about last night, or maybe he was hung over. Bradley checked the time on his cell. Jenn surprised us all when she said, "Come on, guys, Sandee's right. This is what we'd do if we were at a real rehearsal."

I ignored "real rehearsal". They picked up the pace this time and the whole *Our Town* sequence ran twenty-five minutes. With an intro we'd be up to twenty-seven minutes, but thirty-five would be better. Long enough to establish our skill and short enough to leave them wanting more. "Good job," I told them, "and we have time for one more scene. Any suggestions?"

"Are you going to put something in the program about how we're doing this to raise funds, or do you want to add that to Nicole's lines?" Bradley asked. Typical. He hadn't even heard my question. He really needed to learn a few things about listening.

"I don't think we should rewrite the play. Somebody will make a short speech before the show starts. Maybe me. Maybe Ed."

"The kid who plays Simon Stimson?" Nicole asked.

"Think about it. Simon Stimson is a misfit. We're all feeling a little like misfits with no school or sports or routine." I was figuring it out as I talked.

Nicole said. "Simon Stimson's lines have the right

philosophy. Personally, I think Ms. G would do a better job. Or Dr. Henderson."

"Okay. That's possible."

"Better still, why don't you do it?" Nicole's face brightened. "You're the one who put this whole thing together."

Even though I glowed inside, I only said, "Maybe. What about another scene?"

"Maybe Emily and her mom in Act I?" Amber suggested.

"Good," I said, imagining the conversation I hoped Mom and I could have someday. "Want to try it? I can read in Mrs. Webb's lines, and we'll get her here for the next rehearsal."

"Before we get back into it, I've got a question for you," Bradley said from his camp chair.

"Okay." What did Mr. Prep Man want now? Another scene? A solo?

"You know that guy who found us a place to perform?"

I nodded. "You mean Pete."

"He's not in drama, right?"

"Right."

"Why was he hanging out? Is he in music or what?"

"I think he plays with Diego's old band."

"I hope this isn't too personal, Sandee, but what do you know about him? I asked a few people last night, and nobody in the senior class knows him."

The truth was that I only knew what he'd told me, and it wasn't much. "I know he's in AP Math and my parents like him, and most of the time he seems like a good guy."

Amber added, "And he's hot. And mature. And so cool to work with. Do you have a problem with him, Bradley?"

"I don't know. Last night at the Arco station, he was sitting against the chain link fence munching on a bag of chips. It was

175

weird. I could only see part of his face because of his hoodie, and he didn't look up when I drove past and waved. I kept wondering how he knew to show up when the cast met at my house."

"That's easy. I must have said something," I said.

"But when? How did you even meet him?" Bradley asked.

"Diego introduced us outside of Starbucks, and when we found out he was in Gibson's class, I asked if he could tutor me to get Bowen off my case."

"Did you ever see him in the halls between classes?" Bradley asked.

I stuffed my hands in the pockets of my jeans. I hadn't thought about that, and Bradley was acting like a cop, or a lawyer, or somebody in the police dramas Mom sometimes binge watched. He had to be in charge, sort of like Pete, and I thought maybe it was a guy thing when I remembered that we met the day before the big one.

Hesitantly I said, "He was in the parking lot the day school was cancelled."

"Not the same, Sandee. It's like he doesn't really go to San Ramos High."

The same thought had been lurking in my mind, but I never found the courage to find out. "He got us a really good venue."

"Have you seen it?" I could feel my throat constricting as I shook my head, but I wasn't about to lose it in front of him. "Do you have a contract? Better still, has Ms. G signed a contract?"

I took a deep breath and smiled. "You're going to make a great lawyer someday, Bradley," hoping to diffuse the situation. My diversion tactic worked. He beamed. His chest puffed out until I imagined a rooster crowing.

"I hope so," he said. "In the meantime can you text Ms. G about this guy? Something's not right, and if we're putting in all this time, I want to do the show." Funny how a senior could take control away from me so easily.

As we stored our show furniture, I remembered Bri's ease whenever he oversaw anything. Was I being a leader or a loser where Bradley was concerned? What if he was right and Pete hadn't followed through on the contract?

I needed to see the space myself. I added a note to my list: Visit the church secretary ASAP before you contact Ms. G.

# Chapter 25

## Friday, November 1

### Outside Starbucks

After we'd eaten dinner, Bradley's questions still ran through my head, so I went looking for Pete. He sat alone at a table outside the Starbucks where we first met, wearing the same hoodie and jeans that Bradley and I had seen him in at the service station the night before.

Because he was looking down at his phone, he didn't see me coming, so I pulled out a chair, and said, "What's up, Pete?" He didn't react. "Whatcha doin'?" I hoped my tension didn't show.

"Just looking at stuff my friends posted."

"Your San Diego friends?"

"Yup. I'm sorry. This is rude." He stared at me for a minute before a flirty smile crossed his face. "Foxy. Your sweater is just right."

"Thanks." My feelings were all scrambled. "Did you text Ms. G about the rehearsal hall at the church?"

"Of course. Why do you ask?" He waited while I folded my arms and stared. It took him a minute, but he caught on. "Honest, Sandee." He sounded sincere. "Check my texts." He handed me his phone with the texts open. **After Sandee's meeting we talked to the secretary at the Episcopal Church. We can use the rec hall in November, but the secretary says an** adult has to sign the contract. Sandee gave me your number. Here's the secretary's number: 925-555-9057. Thx.

"Very nice." I scrolled down. His eyes grew wide as he saw me do it.

"I only said you could look at that one text."

It was too late. I turned away as he tried to grab the phone and read what Ms. G texted back. Who are you? I can't find you in the school records.

I scrolled further. He hadn't responded, and I didn't know whether Ms. G let it go, called the principal, or contacted the police. I checked my own phone, but she hadn't texted me. "Who are you, Pete?"

He sipped his drink and stared at the parking lot like he was looking for someone to rescue him. No luck. It was deserted. After a moment he sighed and said, "I'm Pete Branson. Just like I told you. Wanna see my driver's license?" Despite the offer, his confidence was gone.

"Why did you tell me you were in AP Math when you aren't even a student?" He fished around in his backpack rather than answering me. "Talk to me, Pete. What's going on?"

"You want the truth?" I nodded. He stared at his phone and said, "I don't need to be enrolled. I graduated already."

"What?" This was getting too weird. "I don't get it. Why are you hanging around San Ramos High if you've already graduated?"

"Sandee, I like you a lot, but sometimes you're incredibly naïve. I'm meeting someone I just met in a couple minutes, so you'd better go."

"Please, Pete. That line isn't working any more. Where are you from, and where are you living?" The wind picked up, and a chill ran through me. I was not about to be sidetracked. Please don't tell me your dad got transferred and you're in some apartment."

Big sigh. No words. Just Pete surveying the parking lot again. Stalling.

I thought of Diego, who said nothing rather than giving me a wrong answer. Now I wished I'd encouraged him more. Diego would never try to hide who he was even if a few dweeby kids hassled him about his Hispanic name. "What's your story? You found us a place for the show, but the cast doesn't know if they can trust you."

He stared, open-mouthed. Looked at his cell. Looked back at me. The wind blew a bunch of stray leaves past us. He grabbed his cup and ran his finger around the top. Looking closely, I saw teeny wrinkles around his eyes and wondered how long they'd been there and how old he really was. "What are you doing here?"

Instead of his usual BS answer, he asked, "What gave me away?"

"You're wearing the same clothes you had on at the Arco Station last night. Bradley and I both saw you sitting there, staring at your shoes and holding a bag of junk food, so don't try to deny it." He sat back and stuffed his hands in his pockets, waiting to see if I knew more. "I haven't been to your apartment once. I haven't even dropped you off outside. You claimed you were in Mr. Gibson's math class, but you aren't even enrolled. Are you a runaway?"

"Maybe."

"From San Diego?"

He let out a big sigh before he said, "Try Antioch. Only a BART trip and a bus ride away. I've been all over the Bay Area looking for a place to live, but the landlords charge outrageous rents around here. Then the earthquake hit. BART practically stopped running. I'm stuck. I can't even shower in the locker room because the campus is closed. I can't spend the night on anybody's couch when I stink, so I've kind of been staying outdoors. It's November, and it's way too cold down by the creek, but outside Starbucks or Arco it's a little warmer."

"Seriously?"

He took a gulp of his drink. "At least there are a lot of parks around here, so I can keep moving around, and there are elementary schools with bushes right next to the buildings. When I'm tucked behind them, it's easy to hide from the security cameras, but I have to be gone before the janitors come in at five."

"And you didn't answer your cell because it wasn't charged?"

"Don't be silly." His old arrogance was back. "I can charge it at any Starbucks. Some of the time I didn't answer because you're too nosy." He watched for my reaction. I didn't give him one. Let him see how it felt to be on the receiving end of being ignored.

"Sorry," he said a minute later. "Nosy is the wrong word, but you've always got a plan or a question or an idea, and I was trying to lay low. Then your dad said I reminded him of your brother, so I thought maybe I could hang out with your family for a while. When I heard Ed and Tony talking about that meeting at your house, I figured I'd stay after to help you and spend the night. If I kept helping, I figured I could live there until the show closed."

How I wanted advice from Tessa. Or Nicole. Even my parents. It was just him and me, so I said, "Speaking of parents, where are yours?"

"Around." I grabbed his drink and took a sip. "Hey! Give that back."

Holding it behind my back, I said, "Not until you tell me where your parents are."

He lunged for it, but I stepped aside. He misstepped and would have gone down if he hadn't caught himself by grabbing the edge of the table. "Come on. You're not the police," he said as he straightened up.

"Are the police looking for you?"

"No." His eyes filled with fear. "My dad would never think to call the police. Besides, he's probably sitting in his lounger, high on pain pills. It's not like he can manage without them."

"Are you serious?"

"He hurt his back, okay? The pills helped for a while."

I returned his cup, handed him his phone, and said, "Call your dad."

"I'll bet he's stopped trying to find me. He's probably too busy watching sports or *Gunsmoke*."

For a minute I thought he was lying again, but his face told me he wasn't. "Oh, Pete, I'm so sorry." I reached out and put my hand over his. "What about your mom?"

"She...um...she's not in the picture any more, okay? It's been Dad and me since June. We were doing okay until he refused to give me enough money for car insurance or college fees."

"So, you're just hanging out here in San Ramos, waiting for...?"

"Waiting for whatever comes up. It's not ideal, but your dad almost took me in. Can you blame me for coming back over and over?"

I shook my head. I felt bad, but we couldn't make him Bri's

replacement.

"Guess I'll find a job and fend for myself. Maybe find roommates."

"What about your dad?"

"I told you. He's sick, and he doesn't really care. Besides, I'm eighteen. It's time for me to be out on my own."

"When did you graduate?"

"Last June. Bay High. Why would I make that up?" I had no idea if he was lying or not. He didn't seem to be, but I'd never seen him wear a Bay High shirt of any kind —not sports or anything.

"I have every right to be suspicious."

He glared at me, then looked away. When he looked back he said, "Please, I need your help."

I nodded. "We'll figure this out together, but first you should call your dad."

He stuck his phone in his pocket and said, "That's not happening." Looking hurt he added, "I thought you were my friend."

"You're making that a little hard. If you won't call your dad, could we call Ms. G to see if she's reserved the church hall, so I know we have a place to perform?"

"Sure, but don't tell her about my dad. Nobody's supposed to know about him. You can tell her the hall is for real. She should follow up and sign the paperwork."

I stretched out my hand for his phone. He didn't move. Maybe he couldn't. Fear can do that to people. I should know after the ladder went lurching around with me on top. "Fine. I'll use my phone, but if there are any questions, you answer them, okay?"

"Wanna buy me another mocha Frappuccino first? They

close in five minutes." Was he completely broke or was I being conned? His eyes twinkled again, but now I wasn't sure what it meant.

"What if I come back out and you're gone?"

"I take it back, Sandee. You're not as naïve as I thought. Take my wallet if you need a guarantee, but don't look in it, okay?"

"Why not?" I loved having the upper hand.

"That's it. I'm coming in with you. Clearly, we ought to watch each other."

We walked into Starbucks together. "As soon as we get your mocha Frappuccino, we're calling Ms. G." By the time we got back to our table, we were laughing and joking together, but there was still an edge between us. "So where are you spending the night?"

He shrugged. "Can I come to your house?"

"What would we tell my parents?"

"Could you sneak me in?" I shook my head, and he said, "Not a problem. I'm waiting for someone. Really. A guy from Diego's band. We'll jam for a while, and I'll probably wind up sleeping there."

"Okay." I'd found him, discovered his secret, and decided to let him run his own life. It wasn't until I was driving away that I remembered we hadn't called Ms. G. How had he managed to put me off again?

## Chapter 26

### Saturday, November 2

### Around San Ramos

The next morning Pete showed up outside Starbucks right after I texted him instead of saying he had to meet someone. We sat at one of the tables under a green umbrella while he called Ms. G, and we used my phone, so she'd pick up. He admitted he wasn't really a student and told her he wanted to help the show because he wanted to hang with me. He said he had a crush on me, and even though I didn't know if it was true or not, a heart-pounding flutter went through me. She promised to call the church, and after I got off the phone Pete said, "Glad we handled that. Thanks, Sandee." Maybe telling the truth had changed him.

After he hung up, I checked the time and said, "Gotta go, Pete. I'm late for rehearsal and it's in our garage. Call your dad. Promise me you'll do it?"

"Of course. I've told you everything. Trust me."

"Call me when it's done?" I sounded a little like Dad, but I honestly wanted to hear what his dad said to the son he hadn't seen since July. Maybe I could help him figure out how his family had gotten so messed up that he ran away. More than anything, though, I wanted the truth. One more lie, and he was out of my life for good.

"Don't keep checking on me, Sandee. You're my girlfriend—not my mom."

That reminded me of something else I wanted to know. As I fished out my keys, I said, "I know. I'm not your mom, and I don't know what happened between you and her. Will you tell me when I'm not late for rehearsal?"

"Okay, girlfriend."

I waved over my shoulder. Two could play the noncommittal game. As I pulled out of the parking lot, I looked back. He looked so vulnerable, sitting by himself with no companion other than his phone. I wanted to trust him, but how could I after all his lies.

Jenn and Nicole were standing between Mom's camellia bushes and the garage door when I pulled into the driveway. They looked like two models in an ad, both in black pants, but one with a jeans jacket in navy and the other in light blue. One tall and the other short. I could imagine an ad saying, "Something for everyone."

"Nicole, any news?" I asked as I got out of the car. She shook her head.

"Don't back out, Nicole. This is an awesome number. We just need a little practice and you'll be up to speed," Jenn said. Then she turned to me. "We were just talking about how much you're trying to do when you pulled up. Can you handle the whole thing, or do you need more help?"

"It's not like we're starting from scratch." As those words popped out of my mouth, Jenn's face broke out in a defensive pout. She probably wanted to take over as director. She could be helpful or bossy and flip from one to another faster than she could change costumes. "Thanks for offering to help, Jenn. Everybody loves what you're doing on stage."

"Well, if you're sure. You called this rehearsal and then you weren't here to open your garage," Jenn said.

I pushed the opener, at the exact moment Tessa stepped out of her car with Tracy. Jenn shook her head and stared at her shoes. "Good, Tessa's here. You two ready to sing?"

"It may sound silly, but 'Wind Beneath my Wings' always lifts my spirits," Nicole said as she set her backpack on our clean garage floor.

Tessa and Tracy harmonized so well that their tinny, taped music didn't matter. They sounded like a couple of teen professionals, and I enjoyed every minute of their song, but afterwards Jenn asked, "Did you find us an accompanist yet?"

"I thought you were asking your voice teacher," I reminded her. "She could meet a lot of potential students if she did the show."

"Wouldn't it be better to have a student do it?" Nicole asked.

"Good idea! Do you know one who plays like a professional?" I asked.

"I can look through old programs and see what I can come up with. Jenn, doesn't your mother play?"

"She's busy with the Children's Theatre." Jenn answered without looking up from her phone.

"Nicole, who's accompanied you in past concerts?"

"Mr. Jackson, but I heard the quake knocked down half of his house. Doesn't Diego play keyboard as well as drums? Maybe we could bring him back that week," Nicole said.

Unexpectedly, my stomach flipped. "I'll call him and ask right after rehearsal. He'd love an excuse to come back."

Jenn looked shocked. "Does he even know the songs?"

"He's a quick learner—especially where music is concerned. It's not like we're talking about math." I turned to Nicole, who was stretching out and added, "Asking Diego is a great idea. Thanks."

"Can we stay and watch the next group?" Jenn asked as she tucked her phone away.

"Sure, if you want to." Maybe she'd be more cooperative if other people were around. "Can you stay too, Nicole?"

"Sorry," Nicole picked up her backpack. "Call me later and

let me know what Diego says. If he can't play for us, I'll ask my singing teacher if she can fill in."

"I thought you and Jenn…"

"…have the same singing teacher? You're right," Nicole whispered, "but Jenn's too pushy. She probably annoyed Ms. Bishop and that's why she said no." Nicole didn't have to say anything more.

"Call me tonight. Hope you get some good news soon."

After three more groups finished, I pulled up Diego's number, hoping school was over for that day. I wandered toward the gate between the Rivera's house and ours. The wind had nearly flattened their overgrown grass. Dandelions bent low. The last of their camellias rotted on the ground beneath the trellises. Why hadn't his cousin's family fixed up the yard, so the place didn't look abandoned? I felt like I was living next to a haunted house with leftover Halloween spirits lurking on the porch. Or maybe my imagination was making me crazy.

I sat on the same canvas swing where Diego and I had said good-bye, listening for creaks and squeaks, as my phone rang. The windows were shut, and the blinds drawn, but shards of glass littered the porch. What if vandals lurked inside? What if Pete wasn't the only one who didn't have a place to sleep? I listened carefully until I was convinced the house was empty… unless intruders slept inside.

"What's up?" I asked the second Diego answered.

"Not much. I'm sitting on your porch. Is Algebra II any easier with your new teacher?"

"Who uses this stuff, anyway?" he asked, which was code for math sucks.

"Math teachers. Engineers. Tax accountants."

"What does that have to do with me?" We both giggled. It had been his standard response whenever he didn't know what to say. Before I could ask if he'd come back and play for us he said,

"Are you guys back in school yet?"

"Not until they replace the science and art wings with portables, get books to replace the damaged ones, and clean up some kind of toxicity."

"Wow."

"I know. I wanted to get out of math but not like this. You can't even get through the caution tape and temporary fencing. A lot of the mess is cleaned up, but there are still holes where the science and art wings used to be."

"That means they're making progress? The old buildings were hauled away?"

My throat ached, but I managed to say, "Yup."

"Anybody doing anything about our restaurant?"

When did he get so responsible? He must want out of Nevada badly. "Ask your dad if he's talked to the landlord. My dad would say to find out if it's insured."

"Insured? You sound like a grown up."

"Earthquakes make you grow up fast."

"Would you stop thinking about things like insurance if I told you how much I miss you?" It was exactly what I wanted to hear. At the same time, it was a gut punch. Good thing he couldn't feel my stomach tensing. Why did I do that whenever he said something I wanted to hear? I could imagine him in the desert, but I had no idea if he was on a bench at school or walking past cactus on his way home or … please, no … with some cute new girl.

"How much do you miss me? Or are you with someone and can't say?"

"I miss you lots. And I'm alone. Trudging through the heat. I'm still wearing shorts in November, and I haven't seen a drop of rain since we got here. I'm meeting my math tutor at the library in five minutes."

"I've got a question. You play keyboards, right?"

"You know that, but I can't get into any of the school music groups until next semester, and there's no outside groups anywhere nearby. No teen clubs either."

"How would you like to play here?"

"What are you talking about?"

"Could you come back and accompany singers in the show we're doing to raise money for co-curricular activities? You'd be perfect. You know everybody, you probably already know the songs, and you could stay in Bri's old room if Mom lets you. And you'd get to see Maria. She's terrific in *Our Town*."

"Wow! Sounds great, but how would I get there?"

"You've got your license, right?"

"My dad's not going to let me drive 270 miles by myself." So, he wasn't as daring as Pete. Maybe he was smarter.

"If your dad can't bring you, maybe you could take the bus. Will you ask and call me back?"

"Sure. Do you really think he'd go for it?"

"Why not?"

"I'll ask, and thanks," he said.

In the background I thought I heard a voice say, "There you are, Diego." Sounded like a girl. Maybe she was his tutor. I couldn't help hoping she had thick glasses, buck teeth, and lots of acne. Her voice kept popping up in my head while I was talking with my parents at dinner, texting Nicole later in the evening, and texting Pete, whose phone was turned off again.

# Chapter 27

## Monday, November 4

### At the Mason Home and Outside

On Monday I phoned the church secretary, who remembered Pete and the two girls. When I asked to see the performance space at ten the next morning, she said, "Sure, but if you're going to use our rec hall, could you please bring the drama teacher so she can sign the papers?"

Sitting up straighter, I said, "I'll check and see if she's available. Can you pencil me in for ten tomorrow?" I felt like my dad's secretary when I said, "Pencil me in." Sometimes little things make me feel grown up.

Next, I texted Ms. G. **Can you meet me at the church at ten tomorrow morning? You can see the space and sign the contract.**

**Sure,** she texted back immediately. Occasionally, something goes completely right. I almost sent her a heart emoji but used a smiley face instead.

Later that day I was deciding who could narrate the second half when the doorbell rang. "I'll get it," I called out as I raced down the stairs. Maybe Pete had come to tell me about his conversation with his dad.

Instead, our neighbor Mr. Garcia stood there. He was only a couple of inches taller than me. He'd been sitting at his kitchen table the night I used his electricity to charge my devices while my parents were in Reno, so I didn't know.

"What can I do for you?" I asked as I flipped on the light.

"May I come in?" he asked, with a hint of a Hispanic accent. He had the same lilt in his voice as Nicole's dad.

"Sure." After all he was a neighbor, and I wasn't home alone.

Once he sat down, he said, "May I ask why so many kids are singing and dancing in your garage?"

After I explained, he said, "I thought the school was closed. Where will you perform?" I started telling him about the church hall, but he cut me off. "And when?"

"November 21, 22 and 23 with dress rehearsals on the 19 and 20. Why?" His questions were making me nervous. He hadn't said why he was there.

"I'll tell you what. I like your idea. If you need someone to run the lights or the sound for your show, I'd like to help." Then he said something that none of us had thought about. "If you use community members like me, we'll bring our families, and you might have twice as many people in the audience."

I figured the audience would be the student body, and their families, but he was exactly right. This was bigger than just the school. We could turn this into a community event, and the donations might double or triple.

"I like the way you think. We have parent volunteers in Drama Boosters, so I'm pretty sure there wouldn't be a problem having an adult run the lights. Do you have any kids enrolled in the school?"

"Not yet. Our son's a baby, remember?" I loved the way he smiled when he thought of his son. "He's our first. But someday we'll have kids there."

"What made you come over?"

"My truck was parked a few feet away while I unloaded it yesterday. The singing I heard was excellent, and I know you had a big meeting a couple of nights ago. You're doing something constructive, and I respect that."

"Well, thank you." I heard tiny doubts in my voice.

He heard the same doubts too, because he said, "I want to help. That's all. I don't have any fancy electrical degrees, but I run a reliable business and maybe if you put an ad in your program and put some of my cards out, I'll get some freelance business out of this."

Nodding, I said, "That sounds reasonable. I know I should be more trusting…"

Shifting in his chair, he said, "But your parents taught you to be wary of strangers. I don't want to be a stranger. Win-win."

"You know we can't pay you, right? All the money we make goes to co-curricular funds."

"Not a problem," he promised.

"Thanks. I'll tell our drama teacher we've found our lighting crew. Your wife doesn't play the piano by any chance, does she?"

He shook his head as he stood up. "I'm looking forward to working with you." Then he reached out and shook my hand, which made me feel more like a producer than a high school student.

I texted Ms. G about Mr. Garcia's suggestion that we involve the community. She wrote back: **We can accept volunteer help—especially for publicity. Only students onstage, okay? It's too late to bring in new acts.**

As I read her response, my phone rang. "Sandee, you'll never believe what happened," Nicole said in an amazingly joyous voice.

I jumped to my feet. "Is your dad home?"

"No, but there's new hope we might find him. A reporter just did a video chat with me, and our story is going to be on at six and again at eleven tonight and one more time on the nine-news tomorrow morning. She's putting the story up on their website with his picture. I'm so excited I can't stand still."

I imagined her clutching her phone and dancing around her bedroom as I asked, "What did you tell her?"

"The same things I told you. She kept asking questions about how people could recognize him and where he might be, and she talked like she had a stake in finding him."

"Did she tell you how she heard about your dad?"

"Just that she got a couple of calls from San Ramos." A couple of calls? If it was Tia Wong, she heard from me. Who else would have reported it? "Sandee, he could be in some rescue mission, or a family could have taken him home or someone might have knocked him out cold. With missing kids they're usually gone forever after forty-eight hours, but he's an adult. Someone's bound to know something. I just hope he isn't starving in some back alley."

I hadn't thought about the possibility that he was injured. "Maybe he's in a hospital somewhere. Wait a minute. You didn't put your contact information on the news, did you?"

"Of course not. Ms. Wong explained how to look at the responses on the website. If anything looks promising, I'll pass it along to Mom or the police."

"Ms. Wong?"

"She said her name is Tia Wong. Why?"

"That's the woman who interviewed me."

"Wow! Did you... Sorry. The phone's buzzing. It's Tia Wong again. I'll call you later."

Sighing, I stuck my phone in my pocket. I was glad for

Nicole. Really. Even if I felt uncomfortable that she didn't know about my tip. I stuffed my arms into my Banana Republic hoodie. "Spike and I are going for a walk. We won't be long," I called out and slammed the door before Mom could answer. I needed to think, and it wasn't like I could knock on Diego's door any more or talk to Bri, so walking Spike was the next best thing.

We were at the end of the block, walking away from the school, when the streetlights came on, flickered, and went back off. Not again. Not after ten days without a power blackout. I sat on the curb and let Spike sniff the bushes.

As I watched Spike nose-noof, I decided Nicole was getting the publicity her family needed. I was glad for her, but it didn't cheer me up. I didn't want to feel that way, but I didn't know how to stop the dread that kept filling my mind.

It was growing too dark outside for anyone to see the tears in my eyes. What if her dad had gotten on a bus and left his family behind? What if he was tired of sales and found a girlfriend who didn't hover or nag? What if Nicole got some awful news in response to the story and it made her drop out of the show?

# PART THREE

Two Weeks Later

## Chapter 28

### Tuesday, November 19

### In Sandee's Room

Dad told me he saw wide-load trucks delivering portables where the science and art wings used to be. I wanted to see for myself, but they weren't in place yet. Caution tape, fences, and chains still protected every gate and driveway. They'd be there until the campus passed a county inspection. I wanted to peek into the theatre, too, but even if I could sneak on campus, I figured it would be locked.

*Revival*, which is the new name for our fall show, will open the day after tomorrow. Dr. Henderson had agreed to introduce the show, Mr. Garcia will run lights, the actors will supply their own costumes, the Drama Boosters are doing refreshments, and we're giving the community this show because our activities matter.

Ms. G sent out a ton of publicity with both of our contact numbers. A couple of Drama Boosters offered to help. I wanted to ask if they played piano, but Ms. G didn't want any parents performing, and I figured that applied to accompanists too. The wrong person might try to change things, and the show could be over before it opened. We'd worked too hard to mess this up.

*Our Town* cast members went out every afternoon encouraging friends and businesses to buy tickets. Pete told me they were dope. Then he asked if I knew what that meant. Duh! Sometimes I wonder whether he thinks I'm a foxy chick or an ignorant child.

When we met at the church hall, Ms. G said, "You've become both a producer and a director. I'm impressed by how well you've handled yourself." She made me feel like a star, even though I wouldn't be onstage. Had Bri handled this many details when he ran Student Council?

I was feeling accomplished until I read an e-mail Jenn forwarded reminding me that our English teacher wanted us to start reading George Orwell's *1984* so we could "compare his predictions about the future to the shift in our realities since the earthquake." I figured the book would be about a region being destroyed by an earthquake, but when I looked it up on GoodReads, it sounded totally different. I downloaded it, read the first page, and decided I'd get to it after the show closed.

Why is Stein doing this? I texted Jenn later.

Something about state attendance requirements. It's not optional any more.

What's not optional?

If we don't have assignments, the schools won't get money from the state. Or something like that. No money means no activities in our senior year.

OMG. If Bowen sends math homework… I hit send. Let her imagine the rest. I had more important things to do than talk to Jenn about school. I sat down and wrote out what I'd say if I introduced the second act myself, but I hadn't finished my first sentence when Dad called out, "Guess who's coming to dinner?"

"Wasn't there an old movie by that name?" I called downstairs.

"Should I send him up to see you?" Dad asked.

"Who is it?"

"It's me, Sandee. We need to talk."

"Pete? What are you doing here?" I jumped to my feet and peered down the stairs. I hadn't heard from him since I told him to call his dad.

"Can I come up? Please. It's important."

"Sure," I said, my heart pounding in a way that had nothing to do with earthquakes.

"Can I use your shower? Then I'll explain everything. I promise." I folded my arms and gave him my best I-don't-trust-you look. "No funny business. I promise." We stared at each other. "Unless you want it," he said to fill the silence and winked.

"You're consistent, but I'll pass."

"No worries. Can I borrow a towel?"

After his shower he put his pants and shirt back on before he walked into my bedroom, then sat on my bed with the towel over one shoulder and said, "I called my dad, like you said."

"And?"

"He said I was welcome home anytime I wanted to come." His voice grew distant as he spoke.

"So, he didn't kick you out?"

"I never said he did. Well, not exactly. Maybe it sounded like that because I hated living with a burn out. He's a loser who won't even try to take care of himself, much less help me."

What would he do when winter came? "I hate to sound like my dad, but how's that working for you?"

Rubbing his wet hair with Mom's towel, he said, "Come on. You know I'm a good kid."

"A kid? Didn't you tell your dad you were eighteen and it was time for you to be on you own?"

He looked down at his bare feet and my carpet, which Mom

hadn't vacuumed this week. "What do you want me to say, Sandee?"

After a big sigh, I plopped down in my desk chair, swiveled around to face him, and said, "Why can't you tell me the whole story?"

"Okay. The police don't quite know what to do with me."

I gasped. "You said the police weren't looking for you." Had he cleaned out his parents' bank account or hurt somebody?

"They found me under the bridge the night after you fell while you were walking Spike." Hearing his name, Spike came over. Pete reached out and Spike nuzzled his hand. My opinion of Pete improved when Spike's didn't growl like he had at the park.

"The San Ramos police can't exactly treat me like a runaway because I'm eighteen. They can't put me in foster care, but they won't let me sleep in parks or under bridges either. The day you told me to call my dad, they'd just given me my final warning," he said as he tied his shoelaces.

"Final warning?"

"If they catch me sleeping outside again, they'll put me in the county jail for vagrancy. I'll have an adult record unless I find a place to stay."

"They'll arrest you for sleeping outside? Being homeless isn't a crime."

"I agree, but they've caught me three times—mostly in that park by the library—with no car or cash or credit cards. If I had money, I'd fight them, but I don't. Besides, I don't want to stay here if I'm not welcome. Plenty of people without a home hang out in Oakland and Berkeley."

Spike still nuzzled Pete's hand, and I knew he was telling the truth. "Once you're eighteen, you're only a runaway if someone is looking for you, right?" He nodded. "But you can't sleep outside regardless of your age?"

"Those are the rules in San Ramos. Or should I say it's the law here?"

"What are you going to do?"

"I'd go to another town, but they put the warning on my record so if another police department looks me up, they'll know. I'm kinda screwed."

"Can't somebody take you in?"

Raising his eyebrows, he stared at me and coughed. He'd already asked to stay with us. Now I knew why. He'd also jumped in and found us a venue when he didn't even have a connection to the school. My parents liked him, and Bri's room wasn't being used, but if he wanted to stay here, they'd need to know why.

Dad would shudder at his refusal to go home. He couldn't imagine a son walking out on his father. Then again, Pete's father wouldn't take responsibility, and that would bring out Dad's sympathy.

"Could you say something?" Pete asked. "Don't just leave me hanging here."

"I'm speechless."

"You?"

"What am I supposed to say to my parents? 'Pete's homeless. Can we take him in?'"

"Works for me, but they'd probably have questions," he said, and he gave me that sexy grin that made me nervous and hopeful at the same time.

I reached for a package of M&Ms in my desk drawer—then stopped myself. I didn't need those to cope. "Where do you go when I can't reach you for days at a time?"

"Away. And sometimes I shut my cell off. The buses only

stop running between midnight and five a.m."

"Where do you go?"

"Durbin. Pleasant Hill. Anywhere my mom might..." He stopped. Froze. His eyes grew wide. He shook his head. "No. I didn't mean..."

I moved next to him, not caring what my parents might say if they walked in and saw us sitting there, hand in hand. "I think it's exactly what you meant to say. What you needed to say." He looked at me and moved to the chair I'd just gotten up from. "Pete, I'm a safe person. Talk to me."

"I kind of didn't tell you everything." He wouldn't meet my eyes. What was his real story? Did he even know any more, or had he lied so much he didn't know what was true any more?

"Last time I heard from Mom, she was in a one-bedroom apartment in San Ramos. Her parents used to live here, and she went to San Ramos High, so maybe it felt like coming home."

"Why did she leave?"

"Who knows why couples separate. Once I turned eighteen, right before graduation, Dad insisted he couldn't pay for tuition or car insurance, so I walked out."

"You ran away?"

"I wrote him a note but snuck back in and brought it with me. Why leave clues? So, today when I called, all he said was 'Come back if you want to.' Does that sound like a caring, concerned parent to you?"

"Can I read the letter?" I asked at the same time Dad called, "You two ready for dinner?" Spike charged out. He doesn't know many words, but dinner, breakfast, and food are three of them.

"We'll be right down, Mr. Mason," Pete called out. He stood up, straightened his clothing, picked up his backpack, and headed for my bedroom door. "I need your help, okay? Let's ask them at dinner."

Having someone so cute living under the same roof might make my popularity soar. "Can I read the letter first?"

He handed it to me. "I'll tell them you're finishing something, and you'll be right down. It's the truth, right?"

"You don't play the piano, do you?" I asked as he approached the door.

"Not one of my talents."

I unfolded the letter he hadn't had the courage to leave his dad. He was one hot mystery.

# Chapter 29

## Tuesday, November 19

### At the Mason's House

*Dear Dad,*
*When you find this letter, I'll be gone. I can't stand living like this. I need a job, a car, and a home where I feel welcome. You keep reminding me I'm eighteen, and you want me to be independent, so it's time for me to move on.*

*Mom might have gone back to San Ramos, so that's where I'm starting. Maybe I won't find her. Maybe I can get a job at Starbucks. Wish I had the diploma I never picked up. Wish I knew why she left home right after my last final.*

*I'm too old for foster care and refuse to waste my life, so don't send the police after me. Maybe I'll find Mom and she can help me with tuition since you won't. Maybe she'll tell me why she left. You won't say what happened, so let me live my life and I'll do the same for you.*

*I have my cell and someday I'll call to remind you of the number, but for right now, let me be on my own. After all the years you spent ignoring me, you owe me that. It should be easy for you.*

*Believe it or not, I love you. Mom too. I just can't live with you until I get my own life together, and you can't or won't help—I don't know which.*

*Pete*

Could this be the same cocky, confident Pete who was downstairs eating dinner with my parents? Was his whole attitude a way to survive? I'd fought with my parents, but I never considered moving out. When Bri died, I'd tiptoed around them, but I always knew they loved me—no matter how quiet or awkward things got—and I never hesitated to ask for help when I needed it. Why had Pete missed his graduation, and when would he tell me about it?

Apparently, I was luckier than I realized. The whole ladder incident was totally scary but not nearly as messy or miserable as this. I respected Pete's courage now that I knew the truth. If this was the truth. What if he had scrawled it out last night at Starbucks and something even worse had happened? I'd ask him when my parents weren't around and watch his eyes. Lately they showed me when he lied.

As I walked into the kitchen, I heard Dad say, "We couldn't let you stay indefinitely, Pete, and I'd have to talk it over with your father, but you seem like a nice young man. We'll see if we can find a way to help you out."

"I'd only need a room and bathroom privileges. Once I find a job, I'll start saving so I can move out. Maybe I could even pay you a little bit of rent."

"Maybe we could let him use Bri's old room. What do you think, Susan?"

Staring at her plate, Mom shook her head. "What would we do with all his things?"

"Pack them up. Share them with his friends and the school. Maybe Sandee would like some of them. I know it's hard to accept, hon, but he's not coming back."

Mom patted her lips with her napkin and stood abruptly.

"Excuse me," she said in a trembling voice. The soles of her shoes clomped up the stairs and I wondered how long she'd sit in Bri's room this time.

"Sorry," I whispered, slipping Pete's note into his hand. His skin was rough, and I wondered if he'd packed gloves. "Dad, could Pete use our address when he applies for jobs?"

"I suppose, since he'll be living here temporarily."

Pete set down his fork and looked Dad straight in the eye. He must have been concerned about Mom when he said, "If I can't use Bri's room, maybe I could sleep in your office or even the garage."

"Let me talk to my wife. We'll figure this out. Then I'll call your father. What's his number?"

Pete wrote it out on the notepad Dad handed him. He didn't look like Bri or have his integrity, but I wanted him to stay anyway. He was sleeping in parks and eating at gas stations. If nothing else worked, he could spend the night on our sofa as far as I was concerned. He couldn't even fill out a job application without an address, and it seemed like the least we could do.

After Dad left the room, I asked Pete, "Why did you miss your graduation?"

"Why does it matter?"

"Don't be defensive. You could call your high school and ask them to send your diploma unless you didn't pass your classes or got kicked out."

Pete's eyes lit up a bit. "I hadn't thought of that. My counselor called me a loser even before I missed graduation. I stopped doing homework and going to class during my last semester, and she told me I was throwing my future away, so I figured she wouldn't do me a favor, but I could call the school and ask what they do with diplomas that aren't picked up. It's worth a try."

"I'm surprised they didn't send it to you."

"If they did, Dad never said a word. Maybe he never even looked in the mailbox."

"And you didn't either?"

"Can't think of everything."

"If you want to go back and look, I can drive you."

"No way. I'm never going back there."

I resisted the temptation to quote Bowen, who often told us, "Never say never." No way I wanted to sound like her. Instead, we both fumbled with our phones. Diego had texted: How's the show going? Call me.

Good. Later. I wrote back. With Pete in the room, I couldn't talk to Diego. Too complicated. I sent Diego one more text, hoping beyond hope. Any chance you can get here to see the show this weekend?

No answer. Maybe he was doing homework or watching TV, but where was his cell?

A couple minutes later Pete said, "You look puzzled. What's up?"

"How long have you been staring at me?"

"Don't answer a question with a question."

I shook my head. "Where did you learn that one?"

"From my history teacher at Bay High."

I couldn't help laughing. For a minute Pete and I were bantering, like I used to do with Diego, but Pete and I had something serious to talk about. "Can you tell me why you think your parents split up?" He shrugged. "Why do you think your mom walked out?" We were still at the dining room table, and I tucked my right leg up under me, so I'd feel taller and more in control.

He was still staring at his phone as he said, "He probably got sick of her nagging just like she got sick of his pills." A minute later he looked up. "I don't know why he kept taking them if they didn't help or why she didn't put him in a treatment center or something. She was a nurse, for God's sake, but when she got off her shift, she sure didn't act like it."

I nodded. For once he was on a roll. If I didn't interrupt, he might continue.

"I felt bad for my sister, Ella. She's just a kid. When they started yelling, she'd put her hands over her ears. I stayed out of the house as much as I could, but she was stuck there unless a friend asked her over.

"It was different for me. I could go out and drive around. My friends in the neighborhood probably knew what was going on, but no one said, 'You can move in here.' And before you ask, I don't know why."

"Okay. So, if this had been going on for a while, what pushed you over the edge?"

He shrugged, stared at his cuticles, and finally said, "Once Mom realized Dad wasn't going to stop the drugs, she took Ella and moved out. She promised he'd relax once she was gone. I figured I'd better stay. He needed someone to look after him, even though I felt like I was looking after the ghost of who he used to be. By the time I asked him to pay my car insurance, the guys I used to hang with had jobs or were leaving for college." He sighed. I didn't move, hoping he'd keep talking. After a minute he added, "Dad sat in his recliner staring at reruns of *Gunsmoke* and *The Rifleman*. When I couldn't stand him any more, I came here. It's kind of hard to find Mom, though. It's not like we've talked. Besides I don't think she wants to be found."

He stared at his hands again. I had the strongest urge to take them in mine and then wrap my arms around him and hold him tight. But he'd misread it and think I wanted things I wasn't ready for. Instead, I asked, "Have you checked the hospitals to see if she's working there?"

"Of course. Hospitals. Clinics. Even private doctors. For all I know, she's changed her name."

"Oh Pete. I'm so sorry that…"

"Look, this isn't your problem," he said. "I just need a temporary place. If your mom's not willing to let me use Bri's room…"

"You'll sleep on the sofa or in the garage. Even if I need to sneak you in. But please tell me why you missed graduation."

"I found Dad in a puddle of his own vomit. I couldn't leave him like that, and Mom hadn't been home for a couple of days, which was pretty weird since they were supposed to be at my graduation. It was like they both forgot all about me."

I put my hand over the back of his. "Are you sure there isn't something you're leaving out?"

He looked away. "I don't think so."

"Will you call the school tomorrow and ask how you can pick up your diploma? You can use our address."

"I'll try, but they're probably as shut down as San Ramos."

"You really think the earthquake traveled that far?"

He laughed, harder and harder, until he was gasping. "Have you seen Bay High? It's as old as San Ramos but way more run down. Trust me. If the earthquake closed streets in the Delta, it hit Antioch for sure."

I didn't know what to say, so I was glad when he changed the subject. "Look, you want me to carry the dishes into the kitchen? We could do them together. Show your mom how useful we can be."

By the time Mom and Dad came back downstairs, we'd cleared the table, put away the leftovers, and done the dishes. The kitchen was spotless. I don't think they noticed.

"Well?" Pete asked.

"You can stay on our sofa tonight, Pete. Tomorrow, I'll talk with your father, and we'll see what he says. I like you a lot. Don't make me regret this," Dad said in a voice more stern than compassionate.

Mom stood in the doorway, arms crossed, staring at her shoes.

"I won't. Thank you," Pete said with more sincerity than I'd ever heard from him.

# Chapter 30

## Wednesday, November 20

### Rec Hall at the Church

Ms. G had agreed that the church hall would work if the actors wore lavalier mics. Mr. Garcia oversaw the process. He had a certain authority despite his height that would keep the actors calm and focused.

I'd run the sound and lighting boards because we were short on crew. Ms. G handed me different colors of tape and asked me to spike the stage for each scene. That way the actors could move like professionals as they placed their set pieces.

Earlier, my dad talked with Pete's dad. He refused to tell me what they said, but Pete's been living on our sofa ever since. Knowing Dad, he put out some feelers searching for Pete's mom. No luck so far, but it hasn't been long.

If this were a TV show, I'd believe she fled the state, taking her daughter and abandoning her son. Life is no TV show, though, and there's no script or dress rehearsal. How could a mother abandon her son, and *why*? Either he really doesn't know, or he's afraid to say.

Starbucks never hired him, but Burger King took him on. A lot of the drama kids go there, even though Pete can't give them free food. A couple of the guys are bulking up on burgers, and girls will usually order Diet Cokes and an order of fries to split five or six ways. Most of them put something in the tip jar, though I don't think anyone but me knows he's homeless. I sure didn't tell them.

At our house he takes out the garbage and vacuums and he's easy to be around. Pete has a great smile, but whatever split his family apart is still more mystery than fact to me.

A day before our first dress rehearsal Diego texted: **Would love to play keyboards. Can't get to San Ramos. No buses, no trains. Dad laughed when I asked if I could drive his car there.** After the text he'd called and said, "I just talked to my dad about giving me a ride again, and he said he couldn't take the time off work."

"What's he doing?"

"Working for my uncle. It's cheaper than paying rent."

"If you get on a bus, I'll pick you up."

"Too many stops, Sandee. I don't want to bail on you, so I'm not going to commit to something I can't pull off. Sorry."

He hung up, and that was that. He was gone. Moved away. He hadn't even said he missed me. Everything changes and people move on. My heart ached when I hung up. I miss Diego and all our history, but Pete's cute enough, and he's living right downstairs. I almost trust him. Not that it matters. Right now, I don't have time to worry about boys. At least that's what I tell myself since our first dress rehearsal is just a few hours away, and I have other things to think about.

Ms. G and I arrived at the church hall at the same time. Together we checked the lights and sound to make sure everything worked.

"How many people does this place hold?" I asked once we were finished.

"More than enough. Three hundred and fifty, I think," she

said as she stood on the low, wooden stage counting the chairs. "I sure hope we get a big turn out."

"Haven't people been selling tickets?" I asked as I went down the rows, straightening the chairs she was counting.

"Almost forty percent have been sold in advance, based on the receipts that kids have turned in. We have another twenty percent checked out to drama and music kids, and we're hoping that teachers, community members, and families will show up."

"How depressing."

"That doesn't sound like you," Ms. G said. "I know you've contacted the Lions and the Rotary, but it's too bad you couldn't get our story on the news," she said, "and Sandee, there's no point in straightening the chairs. The cast is just going to mess them up."

"You're right," I plopped into one of them, my legs sprawled. "Maybe the news story went out too soon. It's a good human-interest story. Should I send it again?"

"If you have time, go for it," Ms. G said. "Did you find an accompanist?"

"Nicole's singing teacher couldn't do it. Mr. Jackson is doing house repairs, and I don't know anybody else who'd know the music. I guess they'll have to use the recordings they've been practicing with."

"What about Diego?"

"His dad won't let him drive 270 miles. He texted me yesterday."

She was checking off something on her clipboard as she said, "I'm sorry he'll miss it, and you won't get to see him. Do your singers have sheet music as well as their recordings?"

"Of course." Most of them brought their sheet music to every rehearsal, hoping an accompanist would be there.

"Then text everyone and ask them to be sure they bring it tonight."

"Why?"

She sat down next to me, placed her clipboard on her lap, and said, "Do you remember when you asked if anyone on the faculty played the piano?"

"Yes. You said no one offered to do it."

"And that was the truth. Besides, you kept saying you were going to get Diego to come back, which sounded like an excellent idea to me."

"Why are you asking? What's changed?"

She smiled. "You know our faculty. Three people said they'd fill in if we couldn't find anyone else. We've reached that point, right?"

"Is Mr. Jackson going to come after all?"

"He will if nobody else can. He wouldn't leave you in a lurch, Sandee." She pulled her cell out of her big teacher purse and said, "I'm going to call Dr. Henderson and Ms. Bowen. Between the two of them, they'll cover it."

"OMG! Bowen and Henderson?" I couldn't stop laughing. Bowen was going to bail me out? And Henderson? This was too much. "Did I ever tell you that Bowen used to play piano, but she couldn't make any money at it?"

"Yes, Sandee," she said with a big smile. "Tomorrow night she's going to help you make some money for the school. She wanted to surprise you, but with all that you're doing, I thought you could use a little warning."

"But she hasn't rehearsed. Neither one of them has."

"Both are sight readers. I think Dr. Henderson plays by ear. I've heard him at a couple of faculty parties. Did you know he was a performing arts major before he went into education?"

I shook my head. Speechless again. "He taught drama in this district years ago. After he decided he wanted to have a bigger impact on students' lives, he got a doctorate in education and became a principal. He said that every performing arts class he took helped prepare him for life."

"Wow." My adrenaline was pumping, but this time it was for joy. "Hope he'll put that in his speech."

"Why don't you ask him to add it in when you see him tonight?" Ms. G suggested.

"He's coming tonight?"

"Of course. It's dress rehearsal."

I couldn't imagine telling him what to do, but I could always say Ms. G suggested it. "With that off your plate, you've got time to send a quick message to every broadcasting company in the area. If we get even one station to pick up our news or maybe get some reporter to come out tonight to talk to a few kids, we might wind up with standing room only. Ask everyone from here to San Francisco and down to Livermore and up to Martinez and out to Brentwood. You never know who might be looking for a human-interest story."


Tech rehearsal started at 4:30. Dr. Henderson wasn't there, so Bowen played for everybody. She was fantastic. She had these amazingly talented hands—despite the age spots. The best part was her smile. As far as I could see, she's way more passionate about playing piano than teaching math.

Her tempo guided the performers, and there was joy on her face. If she'd grown up now, with teachers and parents pushing girls to open their eyes and follow their talents, she might have had a whole different life. But maybe she liked the life she had and didn't know how to show it in the classroom.

I watched her as much as I could, but I was busy taking notes when I wasn't running lights or sound. After rehearsal, I handed my notes to Ms. G, and she gave them to the cast, which cut back on the loud sighs and eye rolling I would have gotten. It went so smoothly that Ed, our Simon Stimson, asked, "Since we're good, can we skip tonight's rehearsal?" He and Tony are so much alike.

"No way," Ms. G said before I opened my mouth. "We've invited some reporters to watch our final dress rehearsal tomorrow night. They might want to interview some of you." Ed perked up when he heard the news, though Ms. G probably meant a reporter might want to interview the leads. "Which reminds me," Ms. G continued, "if any of you have parents that blog or have any connection to local media, please tell them we're looking for publicity. Anything else before we go?"

Nicole raised her hand. "Didn't Taylor suggest we dedicate our performance to people who disappeared after the earthquake? I'd like to put my dad at the top of the list if that's okay."

"You still haven't heard anything?" I asked.

She shook her head. How could she sing and act when her dad might be lying under some rubble or – hard as it was to imagine – dead? "I'm so sorry. Maybe we could add Mr. Jackson since he lost part of his house, and Diego's family. They lost their restaurant."

"Make a list," Ms. G suggested before anyone else could chime in. "Have a good dinner break. Don't overeat. Be back here at seven."

"Can we leave our stuff here?" Tony asked as others gathered their backpacks and jackets.

"We'll lock up but plenty of people have their own keys. Leave your things at your own risk," Ms. G said.

"Some of us are going to Burger King, Sandee. Wanna come?" Jenn asked.

"Sure." It was nice to be included. "Want me to drive?"

"Told you she'd offer," Jenn said to Nicole, who added, "We'd ask you even if you didn't drive."

Pete was taking orders behind the counter when we walked in. Jenn flirted outrageously while Nicole rolled her eyes and I nodded. Watching those two, I realized Pete treated all girls equally. Despite everything he'd been through with his family, or maybe because of it, he treated every female with the same mixture of respect and flirtation, mixed with a touch of arrogance. He was too scared to get close to any of them. Maybe he'd get better in time. I admired his taking the job at Burger King when Starbucks wouldn't hire him.

After Pete handed us our trays and we settled into one of the plastic booths, Jenn said, "How much longer do you think we'll be out of school?"

Nicole stared at the package of fries, and I figured she was wondering about her dad. "Beats me," I finally said. "Wouldn't it be terrible if they closed San Ramos High for the year and sent us to other schools?"

"That would be so unfair!" Jenn protested. "It's not our fault."

"It's nobody's fault," I said. "Or maybe the oil companies are responsible after doing all that drilling off the coast of California. Maybe it's global warming, like Ms. G said."

"Or maybe there are too many heavy buildings weighing down the earth."

"What?" I asked Jenn. "Where did you come up with that? It sounds like one of your grandpa's conspiracy theories. Nobody knows when earthquakes will happen or what makes the plates move," I said.

"You don't suppose there's a fault right under San Ramos do you?" Jenn asked.

"Very creative," Nicole said, taking a sip from her drink. "You should write stories. My mom was talking to Dr. Henderson since I'm graduating in January. He put me on independent study in case we don't go back this semester."

"We'll go back," Jenn assured her. I wasn't so sure. I was going to ask her what she'd do after graduation, but Pete came over, carrying a burger and a Coke.

"Mind if I join you ladies?" he asked.

I scooted over, stuck my backpack on the floor, and patted the space next to me. Pete slid in, smelling like warm French fries.

"Aren't you supposed to be working?" Jenn asked.

"This is my break. I've got fifteen minutes."

She stared, smiled, and asked, "Don't you hate working around all this grease?"

"Supposedly the manager's leaving right after Thanksgiving," he said, biting into his Whopper. "When they move the assistant manager up, I might get his job. If cleaning grease traps helps, I'm good with it."

"What about looking for …" He tapped my leg and shook his head slightly. I smiled. For once I was on the inside, knowing his secret when Nicole and Jenn didn't. "What about looking for work elsewhere if you don't get the new job? Not that we'd want you to leave town."

There was an undercurrent of relief as he sighed softly. "Not going anywhere. Not yet. Not without a reason," he said with a wink so slight that neither Jenn nor Nicole noticed. "Besides, there's supposed to be a nice holiday bonus coming next month."

We'd talk about what Pete was really looking for later—in private. "Did I ever thank you again for getting us the church hall? It's the perfect spot until we get our theatre back."

"Great! I'm not working Friday night, so I should be at your opening." The buzzer on his phone went off. "Back to work," he said as a crowd of tallish girls and shorter boys, all wearing backpacks, walked through the front door. "You three probably have to get back to rehearsal." He was right. We all had something important to do.

# Chapter 31

## Wednesday, November 20

### Rec Hall at the Church

When we got back to the church after dinner, Mr. Garcia was running through his cues. I was still unsure why he wanted to work with high school kids. Maria said he probably had a bigger family than I knew and maybe he had nieces and nephews who would soon be in high school. Or maybe he wanted to get to know his neighbors, and this was a good place to start. There was a lot I didn't know about the people in our town, and Maria planted a seed of curiosity in me.

Ms. Bowen stood with Ms. G and a group of Boosters, chatting and laughing. Who would have thought sour Bowen had friends on the faculty? Apparently, there was a human being under that polyurethane-coated exterior. What turned her into such an automaton in the classroom?

If she were a character, Ms. G would say to look at her background, but I never thought of teachers having backgrounds. They must though. Mr. Jackson lost his house, and Dr. Henderson played by ear. Maybe we could share their human side on the school's website.

Outside it was dark, and the wind scurried across the ground, blowing the dry leaves into a new fury. How I hoped it wouldn't knock tree branches into windshields or fences into pedestrians.

This was no night for chaos. What would we do if it caused a power blackout during our performance?

"Sandee, what's on your mind?" Nicole asked as Ms. G unlocked the door.

"Nothing that's going to happen. Sometimes the wind triggers some weird thoughts. You ready for this?"

"I'm ready for anything. I just wish my dad could be here."

"Don't worry. Your mom will tape it."

She gave me a funny look and said, "That's not what I'm worried about. You, of all people, should know what I'm talking about."

"I'm sorry, Nicole. You're right. I hope no news is good news?" I remembered how tense we felt when Bri went missing.

"You don't get to talk me out of my feelings, Sandee," she said as she set her costumes and make up case on a chair in the back row. "I'll be fine on stage, but I miss my dad and you can't fix that."

"I didn't mean…"

"I know you didn't. Tonight, I'm concentrating on the show, and nobody's going to stop that, okay?" Nicole was so competent that sometimes I forgot how much pain she was in. Of course I couldn't fix it any more than she could stop me from missing Bri. I only wanted to help, but there are some things another person can't fix. Thankfully this show wasn't one of them.

Tonight was our last chance to get everything right. Our performing arts students have high standards, and this was our way to contribute and be noticed. Before I left the house, Mom said she liked the way I was giving back. Maybe she paid more attention than I realized. Without somebody running the light and sound boards, nobody could see or hear the actors, and to help the cause, we had lots of donation cans spread around the room.

I was proud to be a part of the whole show, even though I wouldn't take a bow.

Mom donated cupcakes to the Drama Boosters, even though I told her cookies were easier. "I'm trying a new recipe," she said. Once Pete started staying at our house, her motherly gears kicked back in. Mixing, chopping, stirring, and baking are her new coping tools. Pete's good for her, which makes me a little jealous. Pete noticed, and he brought me into their conversations without treating me like a kid sister. He let me feel valued and appreciated in a way Bri hadn't. They're not the same, though. Bri would never have run away, especially if we were having family troubles. He'd stay until it got fixed.

Maybe Bri would have seen me differently if he got married, and I became an aunt to his kids. Or I made him an uncle. That could never happen now. Horrible the way life screws around with our lives. Even though none of us can bring him back, this earthquake gave me a chance to help out just as he helped his country when he joined the Army.

After Pete shared his letter to his dad, my relationship with him became more honest. Sometimes I miss the flirting. I still want him to wrap his arms around me and tell me I'm special. Other times, I want to wrap my arms around him and tell him he's safe, but I don't know that for sure. I don't know that I can ever be sure about that, but since the quakes rattled all of us, I've discovered that life's better when you put other people first. I can't control Pete any more than I can control the quakes, but I can listen and try to help.

I still think he's hella cute, especially when he looks at me like I'm the moon and he's the sun. Privately, Amber and Jenn told me I was lucky to have him hanging around, but there's a lot I never told them about the boy beneath the facade. If he wants to be Mr. Mystery Man, there's not a lot I can do about it.

The other day Jenn told me I sounded like a real director, which I appreciated. Then she leaned in and whispered, "Are you losing weight?"

"What?"

"You heard me. Are you losing weight because you sure look like it?" I couldn't believe she'd said that. I shrugged and said, "I don't know. I haven't been on the scale." My stomach thumped as those words came out. The idea of losing a noticeable amount of weight thrilled me. I accept that 15 extra pounds is normal for me, but there's something about the girls who know they're hot that I can't fake. Jenn moves like she knows guys are watching her, and she loves it. I know she has dates and fans, but I'm not sure who she'd call if she needed help or advice. She probably craves approval as much as I do.

Tony interrupted my whirling thoughts. He was standing on stage and asked, "Is this right?" as he set Nicole's stool for Act I.

"Check the purple spike marks." He nodded. I felt proud of him and proud of myself for sounding a little like Ms. G. Tony had grown up some since the Halloween party incident. Ed too. Odd the way change spreads outward, one incident after another.

The *Our Town* actors put on their costumes. Ed finished sweeping the stage, kicking up more dust than he should have. Progress, not perfection. I borrowed that line from Tessa. She set up one of her donation boxes next to the refreshments. Nothing stops her.

Half a dozen teachers, a handful of Boosters, and the people in the second act were our audience. Experienced actors will play to everybody and thrive on audience response.

As soon as she had everyone's attention, Ms. G said, "Before we start, I want to say that it's a pleasure to have you here for our final dress rehearsal, Dr. Henderson." From the light and sound booth, I surveyed the church hall. Tonight, we wouldn't have falling ladders or power blackouts or earthquakes disrupting the show. After all we'd been through in the last few weeks, we needed tonight to be a success, but fear and panic often flashed through my head at inconvenient times.

Dr. Henderson said, "It's a pleasure to be here. I'm very impressed with all that you and these kids are doing to raise money and honored that you wanted me to introduce the show."

Before he could get out another word, Ms. G cut him off saying, "We're going to run tonight's rehearsal like a performance. I'll be responsible for the house lights. Sandee, once they're down, count to five and bring the lights up on Dr. Henderson. He'll introduce the show and remind the audience why we're all here. Then as he exits, Nicole will enter, sit on her stool, and start the first act of *Our Town*. Dr. Henderson will share piano duties tonight with Ms. Bowen."

"Unfortunately, I'm attending a Town Council meeting tonight," Dr. Henderson said. "I'll tell them about your show and encourage them to attend with their families."

"It would be great to have standing room only," Ms. G said.

When is he going to rehearse? I wanted to ask. Ms. G never let anyone miss a final dress rehearsal before, but we never had the principal in the show either.

"Sandee, will you call places?"

I did as she asked, and seven members of the *Our Town* cast trooped backstage as I lowered the lights to half. Ms. G clicked the house lights twice and turned them off. There was no dimmer switch.

When the lights came up on Dr. Henderson, I felt the power I had in this job. Once he finished, I dropped the lights down as

Nicole entered and then brought up the whole stage. If we'd been in the theatre, she would have had a spot on her, but tonight, less was more. I brought her mic up as she said, "This play is called *Our Town*."

For a few moments, I sat back observing our friendly audience. All eyes were on Nicole as she said, "It was written by Thornton Wilder and produced and directed mostly by Sandee Mason, who started as our stage manager, before the earthquake, when *Our Town* was going to be our fall play."

A smattering of applause came from backstage. Drama Boosters who'd be ushering or serving refreshments tomorrow night joined in. Two of them stood up and turned toward me as they applauded. Other teachers and parents joined in. I looked over at Ms. G, who was clapping enthusiastically in the glow from the exit light. Ms. Bowen applauded too, and I gave her a thumbs-up. This was way better than the applause actors expected when they took a bow. My heart was pounding, and I felt more fulfilled than I did when it thrummed because Pete was around.

The actors sparkled in front of an audience. The transitions were professional. The lavalieres stayed attached to the actors' costumes, and the scenes from *Our Town* ran thirty-one minutes. I brought the lights out, and then back to half for intermission.

After Ms. G turned on the house lights, I stood up and said, "Good job, everyone. We have a fifteen-minute intermission. Tomorrow and Saturday you'll have to remain backstage, but tonight please stay out here so the people in the second act will have an audience."

My phone buzzed. I glanced and saw it was Pete, but I had no time to read it, much less answer. I had a job to do. I stuck the phone back in my pocket as Jenn shouted, "O.M.G!" from the dressing room. She burst into the house with the newest iPhone in her hand. "Sandee, you'll never believe it. We're on Instagram, TikTok, and Facebook!"

Pictures from our rehearsal were already on her wall. I checked, and they were on mine too. Was someone from the second act taking photos?

Ms. G came over to see what all the chaos was about, and when she saw the pictures she only said, "Nice job. This will bring us lots of publicity. See if they're on the school's page and the San Ramos page."

We checked. They were. "Who did this?" I asked.

Instead of answering she said, "Are you timing intermission?"

"Two minutes to places," I announced. I knocked on the door to the boys' bathroom and repeated myself, then opened the door to the girls room and said, "Places" a third time.

Ms. G blinked the house lights. When they were out, I dimmed the stage, silently counted to five, and brought the stage lights halfway up. Mr. Garcia set two mics center stage for the first song. Tessa entered from stage right, Taylor entered from stage left, and together they reprised "The Wind Beneath My Wings," their soprano and alto voices harmonizing beautifully. The song took on a deeper meaning, and the audience's enthusiastic applause told them they did well.

The transition to the improv troupe took ten seconds. As soon as they were in a line across the upstage wall, Nicole came downstage and said, "We're going to do a piece called Emotional Symphony. We've all been through a ton of emotions since October 3. This will sound like it—or not. That's the fun of improv. You never know what might come up. May I have a suggestion of how you felt when the earth shook?"

"Scared."

"Worried."

"Shook up."

"I heard 'Scared' first. Thank you."

Jenn came down and said, "May I have an emotion you'd tell your parents about."

"Would or wouldn't?" Ed shouted from the front row.

"Would," she said with enough force to level his attitude.

"Excited."

"Exhausted."

"Horny."

"I heard 'excited' first. Thanks."

As the piece progressed, I glanced at the audience. A couple of women with Mom hair were on their cells. Probably their kids didn't do improv, or maybe they were the ones sending out photos. It was too dark for me to recognize them, but everybody here was contributing in some way.

Their being on their phones reminded me of my own, pressing against my butt, but I didn't have time to look at Pete's message yet. I had to pay attention. I wasn't about to screw up.

My phone buzzed again, during the next song, tickling my butt. Probably Pete. Good thing I'd silenced it when I reminded the rest of the cast to turn theirs off.

We were going to end the show with "Here Comes the Sun," and when I heard everyone singing together, I remembered we wanted to invite the audience to join in. Could Ms. Bowen do it from the piano? I scribbled a note and handed it to her during the final improv. She smiled and nodded. Maybe she wasn't as old as I'd always thought. She sure didn't look old when she sat at the piano, smiling as she played.

# Chapter 32

## Thursday, November 21

### In San Ramos after Rehearsal

**I have to talk to you. Call me.** That was Pete's first text. The second one just said, **Please.**

Later, I finally texted back, while Nicole, Maria, and I sat in my car, waiting for Ed after rehearsal finished. Once I dropped my passengers off, I'd fill up the gas tank again to impress Dad, even though the gas stations were closed. I'd use the credit card he gave me. He'd be grateful I remembered to fill the tank.

I was so happy I wanted to spread it around. Happy to have Dad's car so Mom could relax. Happy we overcame the earthquake's destruction. Happy the cast respected me.

Nicole's dad hadn't come home, and the school was still shut down. Despite those bad things, we had so much to be grateful for. We were here and not homeless—except Pete. His problems weren't in his control any more than ours, but we were survivors. All of us.

I dropped Ed off first. He was still glowing. Apparently, acting was more fun than he ever imagined. He auditioned for *Our Town* because he didn't even make water boy for the football team.

When Jenn got out of the car she said, "Don't forget to buy a whiteboard so we can list the people we're dedicating the show to."

"Sandee doesn't forget. She's the reason the show's going up," Nicole said before I could open my mouth.

"Thanks for having my back," I said.

After Saturday's show was over, I'd take a picture of the white board, post it on the school website, send it to media outlets, and say we were still accepting donations. Tessa might not be the only one who'd be running a nonprofit someday.

When Nicole got out of the car a minute later I said, "I hope you hear good news soon."

"Me too, Sandee." Her porch light was on, like a beacon on a lighthouse. Hopefully it would welcome her father soon.

Only Maria was left in the car, and I said, "You're very quiet. Have you heard from Diego?"

"One text when he got there. Nothing since."

"I guess it's good he's not homesick," I said in hopes of cheering her up.

"I suppose, but I miss him. I miss all of them."

"Of course you do, but it's not like … Never mind."

"If you were going to say it's not like Nicole's situation, you're right. It would be horrible to lose your dad in the rubble of an earthquake."

"They still might find him somewhere," I said, turning onto her street. "For all we know, Nicole's father could have a closed head injury like Tessa's sister."

"Who's Tessa?" Maria asked as she lifted her backpack off the floor.

"She's a friend from *Oklahoma!* who came back to sing 'Wind Beneath My Wings' with Taylor. First song in Act II."

"Okay," Maria said though she obviously didn't remember Tessa.

"She's tall and skinny with straight black hair and she enters from stage right."

"I'll watch for her. I've got a question, though. You're a junior, right?" I nodded without taking my eyes off the dark road. "How did you even meet her?"

"Did Diego ever tell you about what happened to my family during *Oklahoma!*" I asked looking at her eyes that were so much like his.

"Just that he got a role, and you didn't. He said drama was cool but tough for girls."

"Fair enough," I said, turning onto her street. "He didn't tell you my brother had been found in Afghanistan. Well, parts of him had been found."

Maria gasped. "Parts?"

My throat closed, but I pushed out the words anyway. "Mom and Dad took me to a Blue Star Moms meeting, and I met Tessa. Her sister was lying in the hospital with a closed-head injury, and her mom ran the meeting. The next day we found out that Bri—that's my brother—was my brother—that he was … gone." My voice cracked. "Tessa and her mom came over because somebody called them. I can't remember who. After a while we became good friends."

"I am so sorry. I had no idea."

"I'm sorry to dump that on you. But ever since we found out that no one's heard from Nicole's dad…"

Maria understood what I couldn't say. "How does she do it?"

"How does who do what?" Talking about Bri drained me. So much sadness in one year.

"How does Nicole keep performing when her dad is missing? If it were me, I'd fall apart."

"It's what she loves."

"Doesn't she love her dad more?" "It keeps her mind occupied." I hadn't realized it until I said it out loud, but performing probably kept her from losing it completely. No telling what she might do without a show to concentrate on.

Maria pulled the door handle and said, "I hope Nicole finds her dad soon."

"I hope he comes home alive. And if you talk to Diego, please tell him I said hi." I couldn't quite bring myself to say I missed him, even though that's what was in my heart. It seemed odd that he hadn't called this week, and I was worried that he was letting go.

"I will," she said, grinning. "Thanks for giving me a ride."

I didn't think about Pete's text again until I walked into our dark house. "Mom? Dad? Pete? Anybody home?" When there was no answer, I said, "Spike, are you around?"

"Woof," he said as he bounced into the living room.

"You all alone?"

"Woof," he said, which could mean either yes or no. Where would they have gone?

I flipped on the light, pulled out my phone, and texted: **Where are you, Pete?**

**Call me**, he wrote back.

"Where are you, Pete?" I repeated when he answered his phone.

"You won't believe this, Sandee. I'm at my mom's apartment."

"You found her?"

"She found me."

"How?"

"Fate, maybe. If I hadn't been working the drive-up window, we would have missed each other."

"What?"

"When she saw who was under the paper hat and the sweaty shirt, she got so excited. Sandee, she was thrilled to see me. Who knew?"

"Wow." Clearly there were things he hadn't told me.

"My mom and sister brought their food in. We sat at the back table and talked about everything. You can't believe how grown up my twelve-year-old sister looks."

"Did you recognize your mom, or did she recognize you?"

"You know I'm too busy bagging food to look at the customers. I didn't even know it was her until she said, 'Pete, is that you under that silly hat?' I recognized her voice before her face. She's dyed her hair. It's longer, but the eyes were hers and so was the voice. At first I was stunned. She was the last person I expected to see at Burger King. And Ella is so funny. When she sat down, she crossed her arms like she didn't want me to see she has boobies now."

The suspense was killing me. "So why did she leave without you?"

"Dad was … um … I guess you could say the meds made him crazy, and he was…umm…doing things you don't do with your daughter. You know what I mean, right?"

"How awful!" I'd heard about that stuff in health class sophomore year, but I didn't know anyone who'd gone through it. Maybe I was more naïve than I realized.

"If I'd known, I would have punched his lights out. Anyway, Mom figured I'd rather crash with friends than live with my druggie father, and since I was graduating, she thought she should let me get on with my life."

"None of my business, but if your mom was a nurse, why didn't she put your dad in rehab or something?"

"She tried. Every intervention was like scratching a sore until it bled. It had to start healing all over again."

"Okay. So where are they living?"

"You'll never believe this, but I'm actually in an apartment in San Ramos. For real. Mom and Ella are sharing the bed and I'll be on the sofa until we figure out something better. The good news is that I'm out of your parents' hair now, and I don't have to lie about having a home any more."

"It's wonderful." Secretly I was kind of sad he didn't need us, but this was so much better. No way he could have taken Bri's place.

"I can still see you, can't I?" he asked.

I almost said, "Why?" because he'd burned me so often. At least he couldn't see me rolling my eyes, since we weren't on video chat. My old self-doubt was safely hidden as I said, "Sure you can. Will you be at the show tomorrow?"

"I wouldn't miss it. My sweetie's running the whole thing."

## Chapter 33

### Thursday, November 21

### The Mason's House and the Rec Hall

Pete came by the next morning to pick up his backpack and duffel bag. My parents were at work, so I was the only one who got to meet Mrs. Benson and Ella. Mrs. Benson was glowing as she stood by her son's side. His hands were stuffed in his pockets, and a confident stance replaced his swagger.

"You kept Pete safe," Mrs. Benson said. "I can't thank you enough."

"He's pretty self-sufficient." That sounded lame. Pete had so much potential. Too bad he struggled so much instead of asking for help when he needed it. He'd lived in a family where the truths hurt so much no one could say them out loud. No wonder he had trust and manipulation all mixed up. Trust became nothing more than a word to him—not conduct that would affect how others saw him, much less how he saw himself. Probably he was subconsciously treating girls and women like he'd watched his dad treat them. In some ways Diego was more mature than he was. Was I ever going to let go of my attachment to him?

If Pete ever got a girlfriend, she'd have no idea what she was getting herself into until it was too late, but there was nothing I could do about it. "See you around, Pete," I said as he opened the front door. It was exactly what I meant, even though he'd called me his girl last night. We couldn't be boyfriend and girlfriend until he understood why honesty mattered. He wasn't there yet, but he'd made me aware of how much I cared about Diego.

A few hours later I headed for opening night. On the way I stopped to get cases of water for the Boosters. Mom's cupcakes sat in the trunk, so I drove carefully. Jenn's parents were bringing their daughter and something fancy for the Booster's table. Ed's parents were coming tonight too. Nicole had texted earlier saying: **Don't need a ride tonight.** She didn't say why, but Nicole would never miss a performance, and it had been a long time since she got drunk after one.

As I headed for the checkout counter, I walked right past the candy aisle. I was here for water and nothing else. There was a time I wouldn't have passed up a sale on share size M&Ms. Not tonight. You can't buy chocolate, even on sale, if it's sabotaging your weight. Lately my relationship with chocolate had changed—like so many other things.

Bradley was sitting on a cement retaining wall outside the church hall we're using as our theatre, typing on his phone. "Want to help me carry stuff in?" I asked through my open car window.

"Happy to." As he grabbed the nearest case of water, he said, "You'll never guess what happened, Sandee."

"I'll bite. Tell me anything as long as it's not bad news."

"What do I keep talking about when I'm not rehearsing?" he asked.

"Umm. Homework?"

He shook his head.

"Classes? College?"

He kept shaking his head.

"Princeton?"

He nodded his eyes glowing.

I gasped. "You got in?"

"Early acceptance. They didn't even wait for my semester grades."

"That's fabulous. I guess three years of straight A's was enough for them."

"Yep. That and my SAT scores. And my optional essay. And all my activities. And my recommendations. They said they saw huge leadership potential in me."

"I'm so glad, Bradley. You're going to stay here for the rest of your senior year, aren't you?" I asked, leaning across the console between the seats.

"Of course. I can't go to college without graduating. Sandee, can I tell you something?" he asked after he'd pulled the last case of water out.

"Absolutely." I loved it when people confided in me.

He leaned forward. "I think you have more leadership potential than I do. I can't believe you pulled this whole thing off. Everybody's talking about it."

"Really?"

"You don't know?"

"Well, I can't exactly hear what people say when I'm not in the room." He laughed and so did I. "Thanks for telling me."

Then he said, "You're kind of like your brother, only shorter. And you have way better hair."

"Thanks, Bradley." Nothing more. No heart throbbing this time. I respected him, but how could I like someone who was about to embark on a whole new life? Then I thought of Pete, who was also starting a new life. Everybody was changing including Diego. I had to accept the loss.

"Do you have more stuff in the trunk?" he asked as he picked up the cases of water again.

"Mom's cupcakes. I'll bring those in." Mom would kill me if anybody dropped her cupcakes—not that I think Bradley would.

"Okay. See you inside." He hoisted the cases of water and headed for the door.

Two minutes later I was trying to balance the tray of cupcakes in one hand so I could open the heavy glass door with the other. It was not going well. If I banged the tray against the glass on the door, somebody would open it, but Mom had warned me that jostling her cupcakes would turn them into a giant mess. I wasn't doing that to her.

A woman I'd never seen, with streaked hair and a heavy turquoise necklace, came up from behind and said, "Let me get that for you." When I turned to thank her she said, "Aren't you Sandee Mason?"

"Yes. I'm sorry, but I don't remember your name."

"That's because we haven't met, honey. I'm Sandy Bishop. We have the same first name, and I've been hearing a lot about Sandee with two e's over at San Ramos High. I read about your show last night on Facebook. Let's get those cupcakes where they're going, and then maybe you can give me a few minutes of your time."

"Sure. Are you the Sandy Bishop who writes the Arts in the Valley blog?" I asked, handing the cupcakes to a Drama Booster wearing so many bracelets that her freckled arms clanked.

"That's me. And you were on a ladder when the big earthquake hit. Right?"

"That's right," I said, closing my eyes against the fear that came up when anybody reminded me of that awful moment.

We sat down on chairs out of the main lines of traffic. "Are you able to talk about what happened and how it affected you?" she asked.

"I'm getting better at it." I told her about swaying, swinging further and further, and holding the aluminum rails while things around me crashed. And how my ordeal seemed small after we found out that whole buildings slid off their foundations. I told her about the caution tape around the school and wanting to see the major devastation in Hayward before we realized there was more than enough of it at home. Then there was the note about co-curricular activities, which might have driven away the kids who only came to school for music or newspaper or football or drama. "We had to keep our activities going. We had Athletic Boosters and Drama Boosters and Music Boosters, but really the programs belonged to us kids, and the first act of our fall play was nearly ready for an audience. Put that together with a few numbers from last spring's talent show and a few improvs and we had a show."

"But you had no access to your theatre. How did you get the church to rent you this hall?" Sandy Bishop asked.

I explained how silver-tongued Pete found this church on a community outreach website. I didn't mention how many lies he'd told to protect his privacy or that he wasn't even a student.

"Are you always this involved in your school?"

I shrugged because I didn't know what to say. I felt kind of shy when I explained how hard I'd work—along with others—to make our fundraiser work. "I'm running the light and sound boards for this show, but we all contributed. Ms. G, our drama teacher, said I'd become the producer, but everybody worked together."

Then she asked, "Do you like running projects and keeping

people involved?"

"Sure. Don't you?"

Instead of answering, she said, "What do you plan to do once your school is open again?"

"Go to class. I'll still stage manage *Our Town*, if we ever do the whole show ... unless my grades drop," I added, thinking of Bowen. We'll probably perform in either January or February. "There'll be a spring show and maybe I'll be on stage, but maybe not. I don't care about that as much as I used to."

"Tell me, Sandee, do you keep a blog?" she asked, shifting on the metal chair.

"No."

"Do you like to write?"

"Well sure, as long as my teacher doesn't get all uptight about punctuation."

"I might have a job for you in conjunction with my 'Arts in the Valley' blog. We're thinking about starting a podcast, and once a week we want to interview the young people in the valley. How would you like to be our interviewer?"

"Seriously?" Butterflies fluttered in my stomach.

She nodded and my heart pounded—not with love like it had for Pete and Diego but with the thrill of a brand-new challenge.

"We'll talk more later, Sandee, but you seem like the right person to take this on and follow through. Right now, though, your drama teacher needs everyone's attention."

# Chapter 34

## Thursday, November 21

### Rec Hall / Theatre

"Before we let our audience in, I want to thank the Drama Boosters, Agnes Bowen, Clyde Henderson, and all the actors, some of whom came back from college, to make this happen. Before we get started, Nicole has something to say," Ms. G said using the mic center stage.

Nicole came out in her Act I costume. She wasn't alone. She beamed with pride as she turned to a man with a bandage over his left eye and a brown suit that hung off his shoulders, linked his arm with hers, and said, "Dad, everyone here wants to know where you've been and what happened."

All along I'd had the strongest feeling that he was missing but not dead. Had Bri told me that in a dream or planted the thought in my brain? I no longer knew, but I loved my sharp instincts.

I looked at the crowd gathering outside. If Pete was out there, I couldn't see him. He hadn't texted since he picked up his stuff. Was I his girl or had that been a convenient line? I couldn't count on him. Maybe I couldn't count on anyone other than myself. Even Diego couldn't get here, though he had a good reason.

On stage Mr. Lorca smiled at his daughter. "I was ending a presentation at the UC Berkeley bookstore …"

"They know that," Nicole said. "What happened when you woke up?"

"A policewoman found me sleeping in the doorway of an old, brick apartment building in downtown Oakland. I don't know how I got there. It's a total blank. She asked my name, and when I opened my mouth, nothing came out. My voice worked, but I couldn't remember who I was. Do you have any idea how scary that was?" I identified. I could see the fear in his eyes as he relived the moment. "Apparently my face was a bloody mess," he said. "I had no idea how that happened either."

Nicole nodded, and I remembered how disoriented I'd felt when I stumbled out to the parking lot after the quake—even with her on one side and Ms. G on the other.

"The officer asked for my ID, so I reached in my pockets, but nothing was there. No wallet. No ID. No cell. I looked down at my jacket. It was a windbreaker crusted with dirt. The cuffs were in tatters. I'd never seen the jacket or jeans. Last I knew I'd been in a suit—not something from a trashcan. Next thing I knew, she was asking about my green card, which I don't have, of course, since I was born in San Antonio. I was shaky, my equilibrium was gone, the words wouldn't come out, and I would have killed for a cup of coffee."

Some of the adults laughed. "Dad, we have a show to do," Nicole said as I glanced at my messages. There was nothing from Pete or anybody else.

"Okay," Mr. Lorca said. "Cut to the chase. When she asked how long I'd been a citizen, I told her I was born here, and so was my father. She ordered me to sit on the curb, and I felt like I was on *Law and Order*. She called for backup and in two minutes a police car came roaring around the corner with sirens blaring and lights flashing."

"The abridged version, Dad?"

"Apparently, I looked like someone they'd been searching for. A criminal who'd escaped from San Quentin. They certainly weren't looking for a salesman with amnesia who had no idea what his home phone number was. I spent five weeks in detention in Oakland charged with being an undocumented immigrant and a fugitive. They even tried to deport me."

I gasped when I heard this, and I wasn't alone. Everyone was talking at once and I heard the woman behind the refreshments table ask, "How did he get to Oakland?"

"So, how did you get out?" Bradley called out from the front row.

"I heard Nicole's voice on the news, and it triggered my memory. I called my wife who gave me our attorney's name and number and brought my grandfather's citizenship papers to the jail. She took me home—in my own clothes—baggy as they are. My memory's spotty, and the doctors want to run more tests, but I'm incredibly grateful that they let me come to see my daughter perform tonight."

As everybody burst into applause, I decided my first podcast interview would be with Nicole. I never thought of Nicole as Hispanic or Latinx. She was a great singer who had overcome an addiction. We never talked about where she came from. I'd barely talked to Diego about his roots either. Weird the way I kept thinking about him. Later tonight, I'll ask Dad where the Masons came from. There's a rich heritage in California, and I want to hear our place in it.

"This is wonderful, Nicole," Ms. G said. "Now there's one more person I want to thank and that's Sandee Mason. In typical Sandee fashion, she organized this whole thing. We know you worked hard, and a few of us have something special... "

Jenn walked up, her heels clicking against the wooden stage, and grabbed the mic out of Ms. G's hand. "Sandee, we can't wait another minute. A bunch of us talked to Mr. Rivera before Ms. Bowen offered to play for us. She's terrific, but we'd already persuaded Mr. Rivera to bring Diego back to San Ramos for the performance. We sent him a list of the songs. Diego brought his keyboard, and he and Ms. Bowen are going to switch off. Isn't that awesome?"

Her words took my breath away. "Where ... where is he?"

"Waiting for my cue," Diego said. He headed for the steps and kept on coming. I rushed up the aisle and we met in the middle of the auditorium. The whole place burst into applause as the two of us hugged in a real, live Hollywood moment that was better than any movie I'd seen recently.

"For nerds they're a pretty cool couple," I overheard Jenn say to Bradley.

I hugged Diego even tighter. He leaned into my ear and whispered, "I would have told you, but I'd promised to keep it a surprise."

"I can't believe you're here. I'd given up all hope," I whispered back. There were tears on my face as I hugged him again. "Does this mean you're back for good?"

"Whenever you need me, I'll come if I can. I had no idea how cool you were until I met a few airheads in Fallon. You're so much more than the girl next door."

"Now that Jenn's done," Ms. G said, "would you set up your keyboard next to Ms. Bowen, Diego?"

"You've got it."

"Sandee, if you'll get the actors backstage, and if the lights and sound are checked, I'll open the house." It was funny to have Ms. G working as the house manager, but I figured people would donate more if she sold the tickets. And they did. Everybody but Pete. He didn't show up. Maybe something more pressing happened. Maybe I'd hear someday. Meanwhile, with Diego back in my life, it was easy to let Pete go.

The house filled up, and so did our donation cans. At eight p.m. Ms. G flipped the houselights twice. The audience took their seats. I called my own blackout, counted to five, and raised the lights. Dr. Henderson came out and thanked the students, the teachers, the parents, the church, Ms. G and me. He said, "Life is a work in progress, and the participants will show us that tonight."

As he went off stage, I lowered the lights, and brought them back up. A glowing Nicole came out and said, "This play is called *Our Town*..." I was as proud of our town, San Ramos, as Thornton Wilder was of Grover's Corners. Our town was real, though, and our people were survivors. I had become as good as my brother without being a clone of him. I'd never forget him or the traumas from the earthquake, but I loved the way my life was moving forward.

# Discussion Questions for Students:

1. Can you summarize the story in 50-150 words?
2. What turning points do you see in the story?
3. Who is your favorite character? Why?
4. What flaw does each character have?
    a. Pete
    b. Bowen
    c. Jenn
    d. Nicole
    e. Diego
    f. Dr. Henderson
    g. Sandee's mom
    h. Sandee's dad
    i. Sandee Mason
5. Why is Nicole able to perform when her dad is missing? What skills does she have? What coping skills do you have for facing crises?
6. If you were Sandee, how would you feel about your parents?
7. How does Sandee change as the story progresses?
8. What, if any, career advice would you give to Ms. Bowen?
9. If you were Sandee and were offered her podcast, who would you interview? Why? List at least five people from your own life. Give a reason why each one would be interesting to interview.
10. What kinds of people do you think Sandee should interview for her podcast?

# Discussion Questions for Everyone:

1. Why doesn't Sandee have more confidence? How does she gain it?
2. When did you first wonder if Pete might be hiding something? Did your feeling for him change when you found out for sure?
3. How did you feel about his lies? Were they necessary? Were they justified?
4. How would you have handled Pete's situation if you were him?
5. Is there any reason to sympathize with Pete's father?
6. Did his mother do the right thing by leaving? Why do you think she missed Pete's graduation?
7. Why do you think the author wrote this book?
8. What are the chances of an earthquake on the Hayward Fault knocking out so much of California?
9. Where do you live? What natural disasters do you have there?
10. What problems have you had or observed as a result of natural disasters?
11. Why do you think the Lorcas didn't call the morgue to find out about Nicole's father?
12. What are the literal and metaphoric earthquakes in this story?
13. Why are there laws that allow police to arrest people for having no home? What would be fairer?

14. How do you think this experience will affect the Lorcas' view on their family history?

15. How do you imagine this incident might change the Lorca family?

16. Do you think Diego's family, the Rivera's, might move back? How might their lives and outlook be affected? What types of disasters have you lived through and how have they changed you?

17. Where do you think Sandee's curiosity will take her next?

18. What career(s) do you think any of these high school students might have when they celebrate their ten-year reunion?

19. If you could write a letter to any of these characters, what would you say about his or her choices, goals, and / or relationships?

# Possible Projects for Book Reports or Group Assignments:

1. What is your favorite scene? Can you cast it and perform it for your class? SUGGESTIONS: Use no more than three to four characters. Use the dialogue in the story. Monologues featuring Sandee or Pete are fine as long as the scene comes from the story—even if it's not in the story. As you act, keep us aware of what each character wants.

2. Can you draw a map of San Ramos that includes the following places:
   a. San Ramos High
      1) Science building
      2) Art building
      3) Little Theatre
      4) Bowen's classroom
      5) Main office
   b. Sandee's home
   c. Diego's home
   d. Starbucks
   e. Burger King
   f. Nicole's home
   g. Children's theatre
   h. Alicia's Antiques
   i. Rivera's Mexican Restaurant

3. Write an essay explaining Pete's issues, or Diego's, or Nicole's. Identify the problems and suggest solutions.

4. Write an essay about one of the social issues the book explores. Some options would be to write about global warming, loss, addictions, homelessness, or self-esteem.

5. What do you think of the ending? Write an alternate ending. Be creative but keep it plausible.